A Tale of One

Other books by ALBERT MALTZ

A Tale of One January

Albert Maltz

Introduction by Patrick Chura

CALDER

CALDER PUBLICATIONS
an imprint of

ALMA BOOKS LTD
Thornton House
Thornton Road
Wimbledon Village
London SW19 4NG
United Kingdom
www.calderpublications.com

A Tale of One January first published by Calder Publications in
January 1967 (the original copyright page states "1966")
This revised edition first published by Calder Publications in 2023

Front cover: David Wardle

ISBN: 978-0-7145-5062-6

Contents

Introduction

Leftist playwright, novelist and Academy Award-winning screen-writer Albert Maltz (1908–85) was a gifted artist who proved himself in multiple genres. He was also famous as one of the Hollywood Ten, a group of film-industry figures who challenged the constitutional legitimacy of the US House Un-American Activities Committee in 1947. For refusing to cooperate with the congressional investigation into alleged communist subversion, Maltz was blacklisted, fined, jailed for ten months and thwarted as a writer for twenty years.

A Tale of One January is Maltz's final novel, and perhaps his most unfairly treated work of fiction. Though Maltz had won wide acclaim in the Depression and Second World War eras, most notably for *The Cross and the Arrow* in 1944, his late-career novels were either ignored or effectively suppressed. When he completed *A Tale of One January* in 1962, the blacklist was still operating. No commercial press in America would risk backlash by publishing a pariah.

Tired of writing under a pseudonym, Maltz held the manuscript for four years, during which he witnessed the rehabilitation of other banned artists. In the end he could rely only on his British publisher, Calder and Boyars, to champion *A Tale of One January* for the English-speaking world. Upon its release in Great Britain in 1967, the novel was enthusiastically received. One reviewer declared, "If Albert Maltz were not already known as a remarkable writer, the first two and a half pages of *A Tale of One January* would immediately establish him as one."

Today the book is even more deserving of attention. Its literary merits aside, it is significant in historical terms as a long-suppressed but fascinating collaboration between a Jewish-American writer and a Holocaust survivor.

* * *

The real events that inspired Maltz's tale have gone largely undocumented, yet they are as important as the novel itself. Among the twenty-two boxes of Albert Maltz's papers archived at the Columbia University Rare Book and Manuscript Library in New York, there is one – Box 19 – labelled simply "A Tale of One January (notes)". Inside this container are nine folders that, when I examined them in December 2021, had obviously remained undisturbed for decades. Each folio was thick with brittle pages held together by rusted paper clips.

The cover of the first folder bore the title "Dounia's Account of Her Escape" in large script, followed by an "Author's Note" in smaller handwriting:

> *In 1960, when I was living in Mexico City, I met a Frenchwoman whose name is Dounia Wasserstrom. She had been a political prisoner in Auschwitz, where she worked as an interpreter for the SS. On Jan. 18, 1945, when the Russian armies were approaching Auschwitz, the prisoners remaining there were marched out under guard for an unknown destination. During the first day of the march Dounia and a close friend of hers escaped. The notes in this folder are her account of the escape and subsequent events as she related them to me in a number of interviews which were conducted in Spanish since she did not speak English nor I French. They form the basis of my novel.*
>
> *In 1964 Mrs Wasserstrom went to testify at the trial of Auschwitz SS men in Frankfurt, Germany. Her testimony was used by Peter Weiss in his play* The Investigation. *She appears there as the "Fifth Witness". On page 75 of the US edition of the play (Atheneum), she is quoted in testimony concerning "the child and the apple" that also appears in my novel. Although I completed my novel in the spring of 1962, it was not until January 1967 that it received its first publication in English, in Great Britain. The* Investigation *received theatre production earlier.*
>
> Albert Maltz, Nov. 1967

As the note suggests, Maltz realized that Wasserstrom's history was worthy of preservation. As early as June 1961, he sent a copy of his interview transcript to the offices of the Author's Guild for safekeeping under the title "Dounia's Escape". Perhaps he knew that the blacklist might deny him the opportunity to introduce that story to the world.

The interviews were especially valuable because in the years leading up to the Frankfurt trials Wasserstrom had remained reticent about the specifics of her Auschwitz ordeal. In pretrial depositions conducted in 1959, she could not bring herself to elaborate on the sadistic acts of Wilhelm Boger (an infamous concentration camp overseer some called "The Tiger of Auschwitz"). Her statements about the brutalities of camp life were so vague and cursory that dismayed prosecutors at the Central Office for the Investigation of Nazi Crimes considered not using her testimony at all.

Wasserstrom was called as a witness in Frankfurt on 23rd April 1964. During a cross-examination by several defence attorneys, she suddenly shocked everyone:

There is one incident I can never forget: it must have been around November 1944. A truck, carrying Jewish children, drove into the camp. The truck stopped by the barracks of the Political Department. A boy – he must have been about four or five years old – jumped down. He was playing with an apple that he was holding in his hand. Boger came with Draser to the door. Boger took the child by his feet and smashed his head against the wall. Draser ordered me to wash the wall after that. Later I was called in to do some translation for Boger. He was sitting in his office eating the boy's apple.

Interest in the "story of the little boy and the apple" has since proliferated among artists and scholars, who regard it as a crucial part of our historical imagination of the world of Auschwitz. Paradoxically, Maltz's novel has languished in obscurity. This new edition of *A Tale of One January* repairs that loss to literary history.

Below is a synopsis of the first few pages of the 1960 interview notes. In these excerpts we sense Maltz's careful eliciting of specifics about existence in Auschwitz, and his search for the essence of the close female friendship at the core of his novel.

* * *

Dounia, a Ukrainian Jew born in Zhytomyr in 1919, was arrested for anti-Nazi resistance in her adopted country of France and sent to Drancy internment camp in 1941. In Drancy she met Janie, a German Jew born in Berlin, who had fled to Holland before the war only to be arrested in France after war broke out. Sent to Auschwitz in '42. The two remained together through Birkenau and Auschwitz, where both worked in the Political Department, Dounia as a translator and Janie as a clerk in the office that wrote out certificates of death for prisoners.

By 1945, Dounia was weak, emaciated and almost skeletal. She weighed seventy pounds, fifty pounds less than her normal weight. Twice she had nearly died from bouts of typhus, during which Janie, four years older than Dounia, had given her food and care. Janie was underweight but not cadaverously so, twenty pounds less than her normal weight of 135 pounds.

The two got along because they were opposites. Dounia was idealistic and philosophical, while Janie was "vital, energetic and practical". Janie teased Dounia about being sentimental. Dounia described Janie using the Spanish lista, *meaning "lively" and "ready" – and "in all ways a very good friend and comrade". They joked that "if both were sent to the effects room to get shoes and had five minutes only, Dounia would get from the pile two rights or two lefts, while Janie would get two matching pairs of shoes for herself and two for Dounia".*

Dounia remembered the date of the evacuation from Auschwitz because it was her twenty-sixth birthday. On that day, as on other birthdays, Janie gave her a present from the packages she got from a male prisoner friend: "a lump of sugar and one small, sweet cracker".

On January 18, prisoners were routed out of bed at 5 a.m. in bitter cold with snow falling, and each given a piece of bread. Marching began at 7 a.m. Their heads had been shaved three days before the march. Dounia turned around and looked at the dead camp in which she had spent three years. Janie was alongside Dounia in an endless column of women in lines of ten, wearing only light jackets and striped prison clothing. Every five rows were accompanied by two Wehrmacht on each side with dogs. "The trained dogs panted at our feet. There were dogs everywhere, and members of the extermination squad followed on sleighs with machine guns. We could not even dream of escape."

Gunshots on the road ahead. At first they did not see the bodies of those shot, because soldiers had thrown them out to not impede the march. "But then corpses began to line the road." Dounia began to lose feeling in her feet and hands. As hours wore on, her feet swelled – she had no feeling, but the rest of her body began to feel warm. She had a hallucination of being near a fire. She could see it, she told Janie, who said, "You have a fever."

It became impossible for Dounia to hold her piece of bread – she could not eat it, and she told Janie she was going to drop it. Janie said she mustn't. Bread was life. But Dounia said she couldn't. Presently she dropped it. Others did the same. There were hundreds of chunks of bread on the road.

After three hours of marching, Dounia saw a wounded prisoner sitting by a tree. She asked a guard if she could go to help the man. The guard said, "Yes, but quick." Janie warned, "Don't' go – he'll shoot you." But she hurried out of the line.

The man had an "F" (French) on his breast and saw Dounia's. "What happened?" she asked.

"They've killed me." He was holding his viscera.

"What can I do for you?"

"Nothing."

Dounia gave him the piece of sugar which she had in her jacket pocket. The guard shouted, "Los, aufstehen!" She ran back in line. Janie chided her: "A Dostoevsky romantic. The man would die anyway," she said. The guard shot the man.

* * *

In this excerpt I stop short of including the details of Dounia and Janie's remarkable escape, which are best left to Albert Maltz.

At the moment the women realize they are free, they are joined by four men: Yanek, twenty-three, a Polish political prisoner; Emil, an Austrian communist, twenty-eight years old, in Auschwitz for seven years; Ernst, a thirty-two-year-old German communist; and Petya, thirty, a captured Russian officer sent to Auschwitz for attempting to escape from a military prison. Dounia is the only one of the six who speaks German, Russian and Polish, hence she is the interpreter. Maltz's notes read, "They agreed that they would all stick together, and that now it would be one for all and all for one."

"If I have to die now," Dounia says on her first night of freedom, "it's worth this twenty minutes of life without SS and dogs." Because they were free, all of them were wildly happy.

Together in the forest for the next thirteen days, the six manage to find shelter, food, clothing, water for bathing and a degree of temporary but thrilling companionship. They find beauty in the sky, in the harsh winter landscape, in the sound of approaching Russian artillery, and in each other.

Among the inner pressures that seek release as they regain human feeling is that of sexual desire. Janie and Ernst are attracted to each other and begin to meet alone at night. Dounia, her body sick and starved, is "dead as a woman", but has tender feelings for Petya, who massages her feet and begs to be her lover. Emil is violently jealous, and at one point vows to kill Petya. Regarding Janie and Ernst, Maltz made a memo to himself: "Note: I shall have to write the scene between them, and all the explosion of feeling."

Sex may seem jarringly out of place in the world of Auschwitz, but it is central to the story Wasserstrom shared. Though it accounts for much of the novel's power, it is not a novelistic invention.

Maltz's notes attempted to explain this element:

"To understand... one must realize that they were not two women and four men, but six special human beings. What was possible for them was not possible in normal times. As human beings they were much more direct, on a more primitive plane with each other, more naked as human beings, than is the custom in civilization."

Among the titles Maltz considered for the novel were *The Six* and, at a later stage, *Naked to Themselves*.

In the text of *A Tale of One January,* the names of all six central characters are changed, but their words and actions in nearly every instance match Wasserstrom's account.

While Maltz accurately related a Holocaust testimony, he altered the facts in two significant ways. First, Wasserstrom, a dark-haired Ukrainian Jew, becomes in Maltz's novel a non-Jewish Frenchwoman with blond hair and blue eyes. This makes Janie the novel's only Jewish character.

Throughout his career, Maltz often chose to de-emphasize specifically Jewish presences in his fiction. In his 1944 novel *The Cross and the Arrow*, he cogently explored the consequences of Nazism without including a Jewish character among his protagonists. Maltz believed that examining the conduct of people brutally entrapped by the systems under which they lived could implicitly create a wider human awareness of social evil that would include a rejection of anti-Semitism. In essence, Maltz recognized the perniciousness of racial othering, but defied representational expectations to assert overarching messages about what makes us human.

Secondly, Maltz took artistic licence by making a telling change to the story of the boy and the apple. The incident therefore differs slightly from the Frankfurt courtroom version. Maltz's twist arguably makes Boger's brutality even more intense and psychologically complex. The reader may judge.

Buried in the yellowed folders containing the notes for *A Tale of One January* in the Columbia Library archives, there is evidence that accounts for both changes. The novel's original manuscript began with an epigraph, a quote from Nikolai Gogol's historical novel *Taras Bulba*:

> *There are no ties more sacred than those of comradeship. A father loves his child, a mother loves her child, and the child loves its father and mother. But that is not the same, brothers. An animal also loves its offspring. But only man can become related to one another through bonds of the soul instead of ties of blood.*

The author's alterations to the factual record transform "Dounia's Escape" from history into literary art. They reveal what Wasserstrom's ordeal meant to Maltz and suggest what it should mean to us.

Patrick Chura, University of Akron

A Tale of One January

To
My wife, Rosemary

Chapter 1

The Escape

1

At five in the morning on Claire's twenty-sixth birthday she was embraced by her friend Lini, who gave her a hard-bought gift: two sweet biscuits and a pair of shoes. Claire, knowing their price, wept. Now, some hours later, she was eating the biscuits while she gazed with intense foreboding at the shoes. It was imperative that she take them off her feet, but she was terrified of doing so.

2

Once, in a world that was a century away, the man Claire married had sent her a bantering missive about her taste in shoes. Claire was thinking of the letter now in a vague, hazy way, recalling not one phrase, but hearing faint tones from the chambers of her heart:

> *Portrait of Claire for Posterity*
> by
> Pierre Barbentanne

She is lovely in a way that almost forbids adornment. Her long, blond hair is the colour of corn silk, and she wears it simply, twisting it into a bun at the back of her neck; since it is feather-light, wisps of it are always astray at her temples and over her forehead, and the slight disarray is enchanting. Her complexion is very fair, and there is such rich colour in her cheeks and lips that make-up would be glaring and would cheapen her appearance; wisely, she avoids it. Her features are almost, but thank God not quite, classically perfect: oval face, high forehead, exquisitely intense, blue eyes, a small, full, beautiful mouth (capable of the most tender and passionately honeyed kisses). Yet the nose of this aristocratic face is, I admit with pleasure, a bit too long for perfection, with a slight rising on the crown.

This plebeian feature is the most gracious thing that nature could have bestowed upon Mademoiselle Olivier, because, from adolescence on, it has given her the sense that she is not really lovely, but only passably attractive. As a result, she has been saved from the cold and lonely pit into which many beautiful women fall – that of complacent narcissism. Far from dedicating herself to her mirror, and to all of the gestures and poses of a self-conscious beauty, she has developed her intelligence to the fullest... and thereby has made of herself a whole, stunning woman, eager and alert, interesting and vital.

Her figure is splendid – or so it would seem to one who has not yet been granted the sight of her naked body – the bosom small and provocative, the belly flat, the waist narrow, the hips generous, the legs long and beautifully turned.

This Claire, this sweetly natural, vividly ripe, enchanting girl, whom I adore, has – alas! – a serious moral flaw. She is addicted – not to alcohol, drugs, flirtation or kleptomania – but to something less accountable and more outré: the practice of wearing high-heeled shoes on all occasions. Let us, for instance, plan a picnic in the Bois* – along come those high-heeled monstrosities, perhaps to be kicked off later for a run on the grass, but inexorably there. She owns no sandals, flats or walking shoes, and I have no doubt that she wears heels when skiing. I am too much in love to characterize this addiction as sickly or fetishistic, but I wonder what someone, more objective than I, would conclude?

One ugly canker gnaws at me constantly: when *the moment* comes, that ineffable moment when she gives herself to me fully and I, trembling with excitement, gaze upon her naked beauty on that hallowed bed, will she… will she be wearing those silly appendages?

To this letter Claire had replied: "Dearest Pierre… it is not too soon to find out."

3

For some time now Claire had not worn high-heeled shoes, or done many other things normal to her former life – brushed her hair, bathed daily, touched the stopper of a perfume bottle to her throat, read books, made love, even menstruated. When a woman's weight drops from one hundred and twenty-eight pounds to ninety-three in the course of two years of abuse in a concentration camp, the ability to ovulate vanishes. There remained of the former Claire only two things that starvation does not change in the human body: the blue of her eyes and the full-lipped mouth. With her shorn head hidden by a kerchief, it was a pinched boy's face she presented now: eyes enormous above cadaverous cheeks, the nose bony and more prominent, the skin pallid. Her body, clad in prison striped dress and jacket, had lost most of its femininity: the limbs had been stripped of flesh, her throat was cord and deep hollows, her bony chest had nipples, but scarcely breasts. On this day, the 18th of January 1945, by irony her birthday, she had been allowed to leave the camp, but the manner of departure was not of her choosing: she had been one of an endless column of ill-clad, exhausted women marching blindly through a heavy snowfall to they knew not where. At times, very faintly, they had heard the rumble of Russian artillery – and not one among them but had prayed for the miracle of sudden rescue, and imagined it in fantasy again and again. It had not come, and the reality had been otherwise: a Wehrmacht* soldier on either side of every fifth row of women – a strong, well-fed soldier with a well-fed, snarling police dog – a soldier whose orders were specific, whose ammunition pouch was full, and who silently took aim when a woman who could go no further sank to her knees in the snow.

Not quite five minutes had passed since Claire's column had been directed into a barn for a rest period. It was one o'clock – they had marched fourteen miles since seven in the morning. Lini, like most of the other women, had thrown her thin, ice-hard blanket over her body, closed her eyes and instantly fallen asleep… not so quickly asleep, however, that she forgot to safeguard her chunk of bread – thrusting it under her skirt, between her thighs. Claire, sitting beside her, was struggling stubbornly against stone-heavy eyelids and the narcotic fatigue that clogged her veins. She knew that before the command came to march again she absolutely had to massage some feeling into her feet.

The shoes, which she had treasured in the morning because her old ones were tattered, had wooden soles an inch thick and uppers woven from jute that now were hard as metal from the ice encrusted on them. They had been large when she first put them on, but they were so tight now that neither had budged in her first weak effort to remove them. She had eaten the two sweet biscuits for the bit of energy they might give her, and she was trying a second time, using both hands on the left shoe, wrenching the heel, aided by the fact that the foot gave her no pain. Twice she paused to pant and gather her meagre strength, and then, finally, the icy heel pulled loose from the iced flesh, and she tugged and tugged with both hands at the front – and the foot came free.

She stared with shock at the swollen, alien toes, at the puffed, bloodless, grey-white flesh. Anguish burst in her heart. She knew at once that there was no purpose in a few minutes, or half an hour, of massage. She knew what frozen feet looked like, and how long anyone could walk on them. There would be no point in trying to leave the barn when the guards shouted "Los aufgehen!"* – as well be shot here as an hour later when she toppled over on the road.

Claire had seen too much death in her twenty-three months in Auschwitz to feel surprise that it might be her turn now. Fear and anguish were inevitable, but not surprise, and not even despair. It was too early for despair: that would not come until a rifle actually was levelled at her. Without conscious decision, all of her powers instantly concentrated on the possibility of escape. The half-dozen guards were at the other end of the building in front of the entrance, their dogs with them. Was there another way out? She surveyed the barn quickly, but in the pale, winter light saw none. There was no skylight in the low roof, no window in any wall. Were there other possibilities? None? Resign herself?

A thought blazed: on coming into the barn she'd had to step up high to the bed of hay inside. There was no visible floor in the interior, merely the hay. And since there were no animals, it was only for storage. But why then was the roof so low? What if part of the building were below ground level?

In the instant, with an effort of will that momentarily overcame her exhaustion, Claire turned over on her knees and began to thrust the hay apart with her hands. It was softly loose, neither baled nor packed down, and in a few moments she had opened a hole the full length of her arms. With a low cry she raised up and began shaking her friend. "Wake up," she whispered urgently, speaking in German. Lini grunted – a hand groped in sleep to push away Claire's hands – and she sat up with a start.

"Time to go?"

"Not yet," Claire whispered. "Listen... My feet are frozen – I can't walk any more. But—"

"What are you talking about?" Lini interrupted hoarsely. "You've *got* to! You know I'll help you."

"I can't... I'm finished... look!" Claire turned her body with effort and thrust out her bare foot. Lini stared at it, then tugged on the right shoe until it came off. Her eyes, when she glanced up at Claire, had panic in them.

"Another hour on the road," Claire said quickly, "and I'll be finished. But I think we can hide here."

"Hide? Where?"

Claire pointed to the hole a foot away. "The hay's soft. I think it's deep enough to hide in."

"They're not fools. They'll look for us."

"They didn't make a count when we came in. How will they know anyone's missing? There must be two hundred in here."

"They'll poke in the hay with bayonets."

"But if we're deep enough…"

"Then the dogs'll find us."

"Dogs can't smell anything through hay."

"How do you know?"

"I'll tell you later, you know I wouldn't lie. You decide for yourself, but it's the only chance I have… Well?"

For a moment of terrible distress Lini stared at Claire. She was chewing her lips; her round, thin face was frozen with uncertainty. Then she glanced quickly across the twilight* cavern to the guards at the door. In a low, charged voice she said, "We've been together so long, I can't leave you." It was not a reasoned decision, and both knew it, but it was a command of heart's blood. Tossing her blanket aside, Lini said quickly, "They'll find us unless we can go really deep – but if we do, how can we breathe?"

"The hay's so loose I think we'll be able to – let's test it."

"Let me go first. If it's deep, I'll keep going down as long as there's air."

She got to her hands and knees, a wide-hipped woman with the strong frame of a peasant, twenty pounds underweight now, but in a much better physical state than Claire. She crawled to the opening and began to work rapidly, thrusting the hay aside and burrowing into it like a mole pushing downward into loose earth. In a few seconds her head and shoulders were out of sight. Claire cast a quick glance back at the guards – and then at a woman nearby, who had sat up and was watching. Now only Lini's legs were visible. "Psst!" Claire said to the watching woman, and raised a warning finger to her lips. The woman glanced at her apathetically without any answering sign. "*Merde!*"* Claire said to herself, and crawled head first into the hole.

The burrow went down at a steep angle. Claire followed Lini's shoes closely, her face only a few inches behind them, while hope and terror churned within her. Would the shoes keep moving? Only faintly was she aware of dust in her nose and open mouth, of the feel of the hay closing over her bare legs, of the blood beginning to pound in her head. As she pushed and slid down, down into greater obscurity and still found air to breathe, she began to quiver with excitement. How deep were they? She couldn't tell. Abruptly her forehead touched a shoe. Why had Lini stopped? The shoe moved slowly, and she followed, holding on to it to maintain contact, able to see it only faintly in the dim light. She became aware that it was no longer a downward, but an upward movement. Why? The upward movement continued slowly... there was a pause... it continued again... and then stopped. Claire understood: Lini had moved so they would be lying flat. But why had she not gone deeper still? She reached out and squeezed her friend's ankle. As though in reply, Lini's shoes began to move sideways. Claire started to follow, but then waited, realizing that Lini was turning. She lay with both arms extended as feelers. A few moments passed, and then Lini's hand, brushing past hers, returned to squeeze it. The shadow of Lini's face approached. Claire felt her warm, panting breath. Lini searched for Claire's ear, whispered into it. "Couldn't... go deeper... couldn't get... enough air."

"We're deep enough," Claire whispered back excitedly. "It's so dark I can hardly see you."

"Oh my God," Lini muttered, "have we really done it?"

They were silent for a few moments, trembling. Suddenly Lini whispered, "How do you know about the dogs?"

"Know what?"

"That they can't smell through hay?"

"My grandfather told me. He used to hunt with dogs."

"Maybe these police dogs have a better sense of smell?"

"They couldn't have. My grandfather's dogs could follow rabbit tracks that were days old. But they couldn't smell a rat in a hay-stack, he told me."

"That better be right," Lini muttered. "God, I'm scared, I'm shaking." She coughed a little. "The dust has dried my throat out."

"Don't talk," Claire said. She reached out... they clasped hands. They lay face to face, staring at each other, every force in their beings concentrated upon the act of listening. Time passed. They couldn't measure it – fifteen minutes, half an hour, more? The gruelling, frightful moment came with shrill whistles and the shouting of the guards: "*All out! Quick! Let's go!*" Both women went rigid, and, instantly, Lini began to cough. Claire jerked her hand free and clapped the palm over her friend's mouth. The harsh shouts came closer, and with them the barking of dogs, and they could hear the movement of many feet on the rustling hay. "*Out! Quick!*" And then a voice directly above them: "*If any of you bitches have hidden in the hay, nothing will happen to you if you come out right now. If we find you hiding, we'll shoot you!*"

Shuddering with terror, they waited for the bayonet thrust from above, for sudden light and a rifle barrel pointing down at them. They heard the harsh voice repeat the threat in another part of the barn. The rustling and snapping of the hay continued... and then, abruptly, it ceased, and there was only the sound of a few guards tramping back and forth, and of their dogs. Whistles began to sound shrilly from outside, which meant that lines were being formed. And then the barking of the dogs also moved outside, and they were alone in a sudden hush.

Lini stopped coughing, and Claire freed her mouth. They lay still, panting with excitement, the sweat of tension clammy on their bodies. They heard the marching commands, and then the crunching of the frosty snow under hundreds of tramping feet.

"My God, we did it," Lini whispered. "We escaped."

"Yes, yes, yes, we did it!" Claire said, sobbing.

"Escaped," Lini repeated with wonder. "We escaped."

They listened exultantly to the sounds from outside. From not far off a rifle cracked, and they both shivered, but then Claire said, "That's me, I'm dead", and they suddenly were stifling delicious laughter, the bitter-crusted laughter that people learn who have lived insupportably close to death and horror. Their laughter exhausted them, and they lay still, tasting the quiet of the barn like honey in their dry mouths. After a while, the sound of marching began to recede.

"We could have been in another column," Claire murmured, "one that rested along the road. Why did we have the luck to be sent in here?"

"Why – why?" Lini whispered with affectionate mockery. "You never change – always looking for philosophy where there is none. Why didn't you die from your typhus? Why weren't we both shot in Toulouse?" And then, after a moment, "I'll give you something real to think about: what do we do now?"

"I don't know," Claire muttered. "I can't think any more. I have to sleep. I'm so tired."

"I forgot my bread," Lini announced after a moment. "That's a terrible mistake. It'll be gone now."

Claire didn't answer. She was already in a comatose sleep. Lini coughed. The last thing she heard was a rifle shot in the distance.

4

In a wild dream, Lini was hiding in a suffocating box while police dogs ran furiously back and forth searching for her. Waking, she heard a new column of prisoners entering the barn. Claire was snoring. Lini shook her gently, whispering into her ear. "Quiet, quiet, quiet!"

With a thick tongue Claire murmured, "Huh? What?"

"Another column! Wake up!"

"I'm awake."

They listened, hearing men's tired voices, curses in a medley of languages, the sound of exhausted bodies sprawling down upon the hay. This time, different from their own entrance, there were warnings in advance about hiding. "*We'll shoot every bastard who tries it,*" a guard shouted, "*and shove a bayonet up his ass first. Don't think we won't find you.*"

Nauseating fear, like some dirty chemical, spurted again through the veins of both women. They had escaped one search

– this time it might be more thorough. A hacking began in Lini's throat, and she covered her mouth with both hands. Time passed – time that squeezed their bodies and hearts in a vice. Abruptly both heard sharp rustling in the hay above them. The sound came closer, and they lay paralysed, like two small sea creatures that have for defence only their aperture in a rock. A man's head suddenly pushed through the hay into their hole, moving so quickly that it struck Lini in the side. A muffled cry from Lini... a grunt of fear from the man... and then recognition on both sides. In the faint light the women could see that the man's head, so close to them, was shaven, and he could see their prisoner kerchiefs.

"What are you doing here?" he whispered in German.

"Hiding," Lini whispered back.

"That's what I want to do."

"All right, but *please*, go somewhere else."

"Sure! See you later." He started away, but then popped his head back into their hole. "Don't worry, girls. We're the last transport." He started to vanish in the hay, and once again popped out at them. "I organized a bottle of cognac!" This time he tunnelled off into obscurity.

"My God!" Lini whispered. "My heart stopped."

"It's wonderful! A man'll know better what to do."

Both women relaxed a bit. That a man should consider the hay a safe place to hide somehow made it safer for them. And that he had come away from Auschwitz with a bottle of cognac conveyed instantly that he was an old-line prisoner with an instinct for survival.

"How long have they been here?" Claire whispered.

"Twenty minutes?"

"Thought it was longer."

"How do you feel?"

"So tired! I could sleep for ever."

"I wonder how long we slept?"

"Few hours I think."

"I'm so thirsty."

"Me too. And hungry."

"It was stupid to forget my bread."

"We're alive. Even with your bread, how long could you have kept walking?"

"I don't know."

For a moment Claire drifted into fantasy, seeing herself tottering along in that army of the half dead through that frozen landscape. How many times the rifles had cracked in the last two hours! She couldn't say what had enabled her to march this far... the sheer momentum of the column, perhaps... and the fact that she still cared about living. Yet she hadn't cared enough to hold on to her kilo of bread. She had dropped it in the snow despite Lini's fierce protest. "You mustn't!" Lini had insisted. "Bread is life."

"I can't hold it any more," she had replied. "My hands are too frozen."

"Then eat it!"

"I'm too tired to eat."

"You must hold it. Try!"

She had tried, but a little while later the bread had slipped from her hands. So had others dropped their bread, their only sustenance for that day and perhaps the next also, and in that act had already begun to depart from the living... as had she. In the last half-hour of the march she had known that she was entering a stage of final exhaustion, of a drugged numbness of body and mind that craves surcease more than life. She had seen it in countless women in Auschwitz as they stumbled back from a day of field labour, and she had even thought vaguely that her eyes must be getting the vacant, glazed look that theirs always had. Yet now the flame of caring was bright again, and it had begun to flicker into life the moment she entered the barn. What had done it? An end to marching, yes... the warmth of the hay and the sleep... but most of all renewed hope. On the road she had lost hope: it had slipped from her heart after the first hour because she had known that it was only a matter of time before she toppled over like those whose bodies were already beginning to dot the road. What was it about the human heart that made it need hope as the body needed water? In Auschwitz so many had lost hope the first days after their arrival and died of one thing or another in the first week or two…

A piercing whistle followed by a yell: "*On your feet! Get your asses moving! Form ranks outside!*"

Dogs barking, the commotion of many men moving, a steady rustling and crunching of the hay above them! Their throats constricted. They lay with hands clasped, bodies rigid, faces twisted by fear. Whistles began to shrill outside the barn.

Suddenly, a violent shout: "*Here's one hiding! Out, you Jew bastard!*"

A wailing, desperate appeal in mangled German: "I was asleep… I didn't hear… I only covered myself to keep warm."

"*Turn around, you filth, QUICK!*"

They had heard many women scream like that, but never before a man. Claire clapped her hands over her ears. A rifle shot ended it.

"*Search back there! Roust them out with your bayonets!*"

For an eternity they listened to the jackboots crunching the hay, the throaty snarl of running dogs, the grunting of the guards as they thrust down into the hay.

"*All right! Let's go! Throw that corpse outside. Good hay shouldn't have Jew shit on it!*"

Presently there came the sound of thousands of feet tramping on the frosty snow.

"He was French," Claire sobbed. "Why didn't he hide deeper?"

"Maybe it was like he said… I'm glad it wasn't our man."

They listened to the marching feet, to the raucous barking of the dogs along the lines.

"How will the world ever know?" Claire asked. "How will those who never saw Auschwitz believe it happened?"

Their sweaty hands still were clasped.

5

The sound of marching had been twenty minutes gone, but they waited for a signal from the man. It came in a somewhat bravura speech: "All right, girls, a bayonet just missed me, but here I am – ha-ha! Coast is clear – come out and have some cognac. Norbert, old man, you fall asleep? Pop your handsome head out."

"Did you hear that?" Lini exclaimed excitedly. "Another man still!"

They pushed up on hands and knees and thrust the hay apart until they could stand. At once there was more light and air. Moving at an angle, they climbed until their heads were free. "Have to rest," Claire murmured, panting.

"We must have been two metres…" Lini started to say, and then, astonished, stopped talking. The man who had called to them was standing nearby, bottle in hand – and three others were emerging from the hay. Heads swivelled, surprised glances were exchanged.

"Ha-ha – quite a company!" the man with the bottle observed euphorically, but keeping his voice down. "Welcome to freedom, comrades." And then: "Otto Mayr, at your service, girls! Haven't seen a girl in a million years. How is it that with such dirty faces you still look beautiful to me? Have some cognac. Sorry I haven't got a roast duck. What else can I do for you?"

"Help her out, please," Lini said. "She's very tired."

Otto dropped the bottle, thrust his hands into the hay to grasp Claire under the arms and pulled her to the surface.

"You don't weigh very much, sister – almost a Mussulman."

"Don't call me that!" Claire snapped, and in the next moment felt apologetic. "Mussulman" was Auschwitz slang for prisoners close to death. She knew how emaciated she was – there was no reason to take offence. "I'm sorry, thank you for helping me."

Obviously contrite, Otto murmured, "I only meant a joke."

"I know that."

Brushing the hay from their clothes, the six of them gathered in a circle, each of the men automatically pulling his round, striped prisoner cap from a pocket in order to cover his shaven head. Silently, with nervous smiles, feeling dazed and uncertain and exalted at being on their own without electrified wire or guards or commands, they began to identify one another by the coloured triangles sewn on their garments. With the exception of Lini, all were non-Jewish political prisoners. Two of the men were German, one was Polish, one a Russian. Claire, in addition to the insignia of a French political, wore an armband marked "Interpreter". It was apparent at once to the women that the Pole and the two Germans had had modestly favourable jobs in the camp. They were underweight, but not cadaverously so, and they were wearing warm civilian clothes rather than the striped ersatz of most prisoners. Both facts meant that they had been in a position to organize some food and clothes in the camp black market.

"So here we are – free!" Otto exclaimed after a few moments. His small grey-green eyes were snapping with happiness. He was a nondescript-looking man, a little under medium height, sallow-skinned, sharp-featured. "Can everybody talk German? My comrade and I don't know anything else."

"I'm from this province, Silesia," the Pole volunteered, "so German I manage." He flashed a smile, showing beautiful teeth – a young, very handsome man. "But it is helpful to talk slow, yes?"

"Not good I," the Russian said, "but understand. Name is Andrey," he added irrelevantly, "soldier Soviet Army." He was tall, extremely gaunt, looking very tried, wearing prison stripes like the two women. He listened to the others with a hand cupped behind his right ear.

"Both of us speak it," Lini announced, "and my friend knows Polish and Russian."

A look of delight came over Andrey's face. Excitedly he enquired if Claire were Russian.

"French," she replied, and giggled a little at his disappointment.

"Comrades, let's decide something right off," said the second German. He was the oldest of the group, appearing to be in his middle forties – a powerfully built man with strong, composed features. "We got away from the transport, but what lies ahead we don't know. How do we want to manage – separate or together?"

Otto pulled the cork from the bottle of cognac, which was already half empty. "I say together. Look at these girls – they can't go it alone."

"Together," the Pole agreed.

Andrey nodded. "Together is correct."

Lini and Claire exchanged glances. "Oh, yes!" Lini said for both of them.

Suddenly all were smiling at one another. "One for all and all for one," Otto proclaimed enthusiastically. "Let's drink to it." He offered the bottle to Lini. "Warm you up. Kept Norbert and me feeling fine all day. What's your name?"

"Lini."

"Cognac in our condition?" Claire asked dubiously. "How will that be?"

"Only one way to find out," Lini replied gaily. She took a small drink, exhaled noisily, grinned, took another. "Thank you, now I *know* I'm out of the camp." Her brown eyes were glowing – her round, thin face, in spite of the dirt smudges on it, was shining with joy.

"To hear a woman's voice – that tells us men *we're* out of the camp, eh?" remarked Otto. He extended the bottle to Claire. "Your name?"

"Claire." She took a tiny sip, returned the bottle.

"That didn't even wet your mouth."

"I'm afraid to take more."

"Is correct," Andrey put in.

Otto chuckled and passed the bottle to the Pole. "Who are you?"

"Jurek… Thank you." He swallowed a mouthful with deep pleasure.

"I'm Norbert," said the second German. He spoke with controlled tension. "Let's take stock. What food have we got?" He pulled a small piece of dark bread from one pocket of his short jacket. "That's all I have." He accepted the bottle from Jurek and drank quickly.

"We have nothing," Claire stated.

Jurek extended empty palms.

Andrey, taking the bottle, opened his jacket and pulled out a small chunk of bread. He drank eagerly and, quite evidently, restrained himself from drinking more than his share. "Ah, *spasibo*,"* he exclaimed hoarsely, returning the bottle to Otto.

"Well, Otto," Norbert enquired, "you organize anything good from the kitchen?"

Otto hesitated. The pause was so brief that it was almost unnoticeable, but each of the others, honed to sharpness by camp life, marked it. He took a second too long to drink, to examine the bottle as he corked it. "Not enough to take us far." He pulled half a pound of horse-meat sausage from one pocket of his leather jacket, a bit of bread and a paper bag from the other. "Lump sugar," he announced with pride.

"Lump sugar," Lini repeated rather thickly. "Impossible, doesn't exist." She swayed, sat down heavily and burst into merry laughter. "I'm drunk. It feels good."

In the instant all were laughing, shaking with laughter, as though they never before had seen anything so comic. Within seconds, however, Norbert's laughter stopped as though someone had struck him in the face, and both of his arms shot out in a violent gesture. "Sh! Quiet!" All but Lini responded, and Norbert shook her. "Stop it, girl. Quiet!"

"Excuse me." She controlled her mirth, but continued to giggle softly and happily. Claire sat down and put an arm around her.

"What's the matter with us?" Norbert asked. "We're not on the moon. There could be an SS troop right outside. We've got to keep our wits about us."

"*Da, da!*"* Andrey whispered, very perturbed. "Was crazy laugh like that."

Otto, still grinning, observed with relish, "To escape the march, to be alive, that's crazy! Inside me I want to yell, dance, sing, get drunk, kiss everybody. Jesus Christ, we're free!"

"Sure," Norbert agreed, "but we've got to keep our wits about us, or we won't be. Now listen, everyone: nothing to eat, and we've got to stay in hiding till the Russians come. How do we manage that?"

"By myself earlier," Jurek spoke up, "I was thinking like so: I am Pole. I go to the farmer belongs this barn. He is a Pole, too. I ask him for food, to hide me. So now I go speak for all, yes?"

"*Nyet!*"* Andrey burst out emphatically, a hand behind his ear. "Farmer is collaborator, suppose. What happen? He tell Germans. We shot."

A discussion began in which Andrey found no support, because he had no alternative plan. He was voted down. He accepted the decision with a look of foreboding.

"*Wszystko będzie dobrze,*" Jurek said with his flashing smile to Andrey. "That mean in Polish everything will go all right." He went to the door, pushed it open a few inches and peered out. He opened it wider and surveyed all around. From inside they could see a strip of yard with a corner of a two-storey house beyond. Jurek slipped out, closing the door behind him.

"It's stopped snowing," Claire murmured.

"Stopped?" asked Norbert. He looked at her queerly. "Was there snow when you were marching?"

"All day."

Norbert exchanged glances with the others. "After your transport left here, what did you do?"

"Slept."

"Until we came?"

Claire nodded.

"You didn't wake up in between?"

"No. Why?"

The look in Norbert's pale-blue eyes was one of pure pity. "You girls slept two days."

Lini raised her head from Claire's shoulder. "What's that?"

"It was snowing hard when the first transports left on the eighteenth. It hasn't snowed since. Today's the twentieth."

Claire and Lini gazed at each other. Claire smiled wanly. "I could sleep for two years."

"Say, girls," Otto asked, "what made you hide? Nobody else in your transport did."

"I couldn't march any more," Claire answered. "It was my only chance. Lini decided to stay with me because" – she smiled – "because she's Lini."

"Come to think of it," Otto continued, "why didn't more men try it? Why only us four?"

"I don't know about the men," Lini said, "but most of the women were so exhausted they dropped on the hay and went to sleep. That's what I did. If not for Claire, I would've slept until the guards got us up."

"The same with the men," Norbert put in. "Too tired even to think. Anyway, most had the idea of escape beaten out of them long ago. The Nazis are expert at that."

"What about you two?" Lini asked. "Weren't you just as tired?"

"Otto and me are long-timers. We ate better than most and started out in better shape. We decided to run at the first chance because we knew it would be a death march in weather like this."

"And you?" Claire asked Andrey.

"With me is always idea for escape," he answered matter-of-factly. "Is my…" He paused, searching for a word, and then spoke to Claire in Russian.

"It's his psychology," Claire translated. "After he was captured, he escaped from a prisoner-of-war camp."

"You don't say!" Otto exclaimed admiringly. And then, with sudden excitement, "When were you captured?"

"Is seven months now. Last year July."

"Do you know if the Americans and British are fighting in France?"

"Is so. Invade there before I am capture."

"I told you!" Otto burst out gleefully to Norbert. "You've been in so long you don't believe anything you hear."

Norbert shrugged and smiled. "So Hitler's getting licked in the east and the west both, eh?" he asked happily.

"Licked? What is?"

"Defeated."

"Oh, yes! This year, I think, is finish."

"I'm quite sure the Allies are in Germany already," Claire volunteered. "I heard some Gestapo officers talking about it."

Otto pulled out the cognac bottle. "Not too much left, but news like this calls for a drink. You first, Lini, eh?"

Lini laughed and waved him away.

"*Nyet*," said Andrey. "More I am not able. Thank you."

Extending the bottle to Norbert, Otto nudged him, and they moved away from the others.

"If we don't get grub from the farmer, what do we do?"

Norbert shrugged. "We'll decide then."

Otto's long, sharp features set hard. "I didn't live through seven years of hell to starve to death now." He reached into his trouser pocket and pulled out a long-bladed German army knife wrapped in a rag. With a thin grin he said, "Our kitchen capo bought this from an SS man last week. I stole it from him yesterday."

"So what?"

"That Polack better give us something to eat, eh?"

"Put it away."

"You haven't answered me."

"Yes, I have. I said 'put it away'. We're not fascists, are we?"

"Oh, horseshit!" With a grimace Otto walked off. Norbert began pacing up and down.

6

In Russian Andrey asked Claire deferentially, "May I sit by you?"

"Of course."

"I'm curious to know…" He stopped and leant forward. "Your feet are frozen!"

Claire nodded.

"But you should be working on them. It's very dangerous for you."

"I know that, but I forgot about them until you reminded me. I've been too happy."

"Permit me!" He pressed the flesh of one foot. "After two days indoors you still have no pain?"

"Is that a bad sign?"

He ignored the question. "You must begin massage at once! Start where your leg joins the trunk – massage downward. But don't touch the foot."

"Thank you. I'll do it, but I don't know how long I can keep it up. I'm quite weak."

"It would be better anyway if someone else did it for you. If your friend isn't strong enough, then one of us. You mustn't have shame about it. There must be steady massage from now on."

"Would it be good to rub my feet with snow?"

"No, a wrong treatment. Very bad. Is your friend too dizzy to begin now?"

Claire spoke to Lini, who raised her head.

"I'm all right, I can do it. But, God, I'm so thirsty! Couldn't we get some snow to eat?"

In German Andrey said, "Is not correct us go outside. You wait Jurek, ask him water." Then to Claire in Russian: "Tell her how to do it."

He listened, a hand behind his ear, and watched with care as Lini sat down in front of Claire and took her left leg on her lap. As Lini began to lift Claire's dress and the shoddy ersatz slip beneath it, Claire felt a flush of embarrassment go through her – and instantly knew why. When she entered Auschwitz, she had been shaven, stripped and tattooed by the women inmates in charge – and all of it in front of several male guards – yet she had not felt shame because she did not regard an SS man as a human being. That she felt unease now was the result of being in the real world again, with a real man's eyes upon her, and she was embarrassed – not at the exposure of her leg, but at its lack of normal femininity. "I'm beginning to feel like a woman again," she thought, and there was a sudden tremor in her heart.

"This way?" Lini asked Andrey.

"Yes, and like so." He gestured.

Otto moved close and stood watching. "You march barefoot?"

"No, but I took off my shoes when we came in here."

"Where did you leave them?"

"About there."

"Please," Lini added, "when we went into the hay, we left our blankets, too, and my kilo of bread. Maybe…"

"I'll look."

Andrey said to Claire: "So, now… how is it you know Russian?"

"My grandfather was born in Russia, my grandmother in Poland. They taught me, and I studied Russian at the Sorbonne. That's a university."

"But of course," Andrey remarked with a smile, "the Sorbonne is a university, not the name of a borsch.* You thought I wouldn't know?"

Claire smiled, then murmured, "We're strangers."

"And Debussy* is not a cheese," Andrey went on in gentle mockery. He suddenly began to hum a theme. With surprise and interest Claire listened.

Otto returned saying, "No shoes, no blankets, no bread."

"Sh!" Andrey smiled. "Debussy for French comrade." Beating with his finger, he continued to hum. He broke off as the door opened noisily. All, instantly tense, watched Jurek come towards them. He had a pencil and paper in his hand.

"Well?" asked Norbert.

"He will give us to eat. But to hide here, no. It is too dangerous – this is important road. We must go away tonight."

Silence!

"He's right," Norbert said decisively. "Did he tell you where we can go?"

"Is little village, Stara Wieś,* on other side of woods."

"Far?" Claire enquired with anxiety.

"Three kilometres."

"Does he know anyone in the village who'll hide us?" Otto asked.

Jurek shrugged. "We will see there… Is one thing he want from us. We write in Russian that he save six prisoners escape from Auschwitz. We sign names and put numbers."

Andrey laughed sourly. "You see? Collaborator! He no save us, we do it. Maybe not even village where he says is village. I hope my comrades hang him."

Again an argument broke out, with Andrey standing alone. It was agreed that they had no choice. Muttering his displeasure, Andrey took the pencil and began writing the statement. Otto suddenly knelt by Claire and whispered, "You know Russian. See that it's right – no tricks." When her turn came to sign, Claire paused to read it, added her name and number and nodded to Otto.

As Jurek started out, Norbert said, "Wait. Ask him for something else." He gestured to Andrey and the two women. "They need different clothes. She needs shoes."

"And water," Lini added. "Please, some water."

Jurek gestured and went out.

Andrey said in Russian to Claire, "If the collaborator has no shoes for you, don't worry. I will make you boots from hay."

"How?"

"You'll see. Tell your friend to massage the right leg now. She should keep changing every five minutes."

As Lini shifted her position, Andrey nudged Otto and moved his head slightly. Together they walked over to Norbert, who was sprawled out, chewing a piece of hay, frowning in thought. Andrey spoke in a low voice: "Listen, please: French girl is weak like baby. Both girls need extra eat." To Otto: "You give them sausage, yes? Is correct!"

Again there was a split second of hesitation on Otto's part. "I guess so, sure. What do you say, Norbert?"

"It's a good idea, but" – to Andrey – "what about you?" With a little smile: "You're not so far from a Mussulman yourself."

Andrey shook his head. "Now I free I get strong quick. No more field commando." He grinned.

"Maybe we better ask Jurek first," Otto put in.

The door opened.

"So ask him," said Norbert.

Jurek, carrying a pail of water with a dipper in it, was followed by a tall, heavy-set farmer of fifty wearing a dirty sheepskin coat. He looked grim and worried as he surveyed his guests. Norbert stood up, went over to him and offered his hand, saying "Thank you" in Polish. The farmer shook his hand, nodded, remained silent. He pointed to Andrey and Claire, and spoke rapidly to Jurek in a hoarse voice. Then he went out. Jurek interpreted: "Clothes for Andrey he has, for Claire maybe, for Lini no. I go bring them."

Otto touched his arm and asked about the sausage. Nodding assent, Jurek added that the farmer's woman was starting to make a potato soup, and it would be best to save most of the sausage for later.

Claire and Lini were still quenching their thirst, alternating with the dipper, as the men went up to them.

"Well, girls," Otto announced heartily, "we men have decided you need fattening up. So" – he took the sausage and the knife from his pockets – "this is only for you."

"And a little bread, too," added Norbert. "You girls haven't eaten for two days." He gave Lini the piece of bread he had saved from the march. Silently Andrey extended his to Claire.

Both women protested that they wanted everything to be shared equally.

"Overruled by majority decision. You don't know how good it is to look at a woman." He cut each of them a thick slice. "No more now, because there's soup being made."

"So then," Lini said with a warm smile, "all we can do is thank you."

Claire, staring at the bread and sausage in her hand, began to cry.

"What's the matter?" asked Otto.

"It's the first time in two years men have been kind to us."

"Ach," Lini exclaimed as she chewed the sausage hungrily, "so why doesn't it make you feel good? Always such a romantic! Only somebody like you could cry over it!"

Chapter 2

The Factory

I

In the late afternoon, when it was dark, they left the barn in pairs – Jurek and Norbert in front, the two women fifteen yards behind, Andrey and Otto at the rear. Although Lini still was wearing her prison stripes, Andrey and Claire had civilian clothes. Both looked odd in their new garments. Claire had been given the corduroy trousers, flannel shirt, sweater and felt-lined jacket of a fourteen-year-old boy who evidently had been thin and gangling – the farmer's son, it turned out, who had died the previous year. She was delighted with the clothes, because they were warm and fitted surprisingly well, but she looked so much the undernourished, adolescent boy in them that the kerchief on her head seemed absurd. In sharp contrast, Andrey was wearing work-stained garments the farmer had used for a decade. They were vastly large for his hungry frame, had rents in them and had been patched again and again with different-coloured scraps of cloth. He looked half scarecrow, half clown. There had been another explosion of laughter when the two had changed.

As soon as they left the barn, they crossed the road and entered a wood that bordered it. All were tense, silent, fearful. Imprisonment had become so much their natural state that the dark wood was immediately peopled with phantoms – foully grinning SS guards ready to loose dogs upon them – those monstrous dogs trained to viciousness, eager to mangle face and thigh and the genitals of men. Yet, apprehensive as they were, all were feverish with excitement, elation, hope. They *had* escaped – they *were* free!

For Claire's sake, as well as for reasons of caution, they went quite slowly. The shoes of the dead lad had been several sizes too large, and Andrey had fashioned the boots he had promised. He had moulded thickness after thickness of hay around Claire's ankles and feet, tying them fast with strands of hay twisted together. Claire had been afraid the boots would go to pieces, but she found that they held up well in walking on snow, and their warm softness was a blessing, because her feet had begun to hurt her.

Jurek led them, as the farmer had directed, at an angle through the wood towards the town they hoped would be there. They saw no one, came upon no footprints in the snow, and heard no sounds other than the frosty crackle under their feet and, occasionally, a very faint rumbling of artillery behind them. The snow was not over six inches deep in most places, and walking was not difficult, but it was very cold, and all of them suffered from it. Yet, however much it punished their bodies, they endured it with automatic stoicism and without dwelling upon it. Their spirits had learnt accommodation to much more than cold: to incessant hunger and unending fear, to the horrible stench of human bodies burning in crematoria, and to all of the abuse to which a human being can be subjected and still survive. It made for a strong and bitter bond amongst them.

The moon rose early, full and luminous. As its bright rays began to penetrate the wood, their tensions lessened, but they still maintained silence. They had been walking an hour when the trees began to thin out. After another ten minutes, the two in front halted. The others joined them, and Jurek pointed. Seventy-five yards off was a large, two-storey brick building. "We there," he whispered. "Farmer told me is empty factory where is village." All of them turned with elated grins to Andrey, who gestured sheepishly. Despite the gift of clothes and a good meal, Andrey had kept insisting that the farmer could not be trusted.

"Stay here," said Jurek. He was rubbing his ears to warm them. "I go look."

"Careful," Norbert warned.

Jurek smiled and gestured with airy confidence. "This my country. *Wszystko będzie dobrze*."

"Wait!" Lini burst out, catching his arm. "What's the matter with us?" She pointed to the prisoner's insignia on Jurek's coat and then to his striped cap.

"Damn it!" Norbert exclaimed for all of them, "We've been prisoners so long we didn't notice. We've got to keep our wits about us."

"No harm done," Lini said cheerfully.

As Otto set to work to cut the red triangles from Jurek's jacket, shirt and trousers, Claire said to the men, "You don't know yet how practical Lini is. If they gave us two minutes in the Effects Room to get shoes, I'd pull two left shoes out of the pile, but Lini would come back with matching pairs for her and me both."

"Naturally!" Lini commented. "The Dutch are good housekeepers. That's why Amsterdam is cleaner than Paris."

"And more beautiful," Claire added.

"Of course!"

"Claire," Andrey whispered in Russian, "how are your feet?"

"Hurting."

"Much?"

"A steady ache."

"I'm sorry you have pain, but it means there's circulation again. It's good."

"Then I'm glad."

"Was the walk hard for you?"

"I'm tired, but the soup helped me a lot."

"And being free, I think, eh?"

Claire smiled at him, and nodded. "Andrey, why were you so suspicious of that farmer? He treated us very well."

"I was wrong about him, I admit it with pleasure. But I had a bad experience when I escaped from the prisoner-of-war camp. After three days without food, I had to go to a farmhouse. I went at night, of course. The farmer fed me and put me to bed – and in the morning the SS were there."

Otto waved the three red triangles in front of Jurek's nose. "You want me to save them for you – a memento of Auschwitz?"

Jurek grinned as he put his cap in his pocket. "Are ladies here. I cannot speak my mind."

They watched him start for the factory, hands in his pockets, head up, as though he were on his home territory.

"Please," Lini whispered anxiously to the night, "no soldiers!"

The naked field between them and the factory was flooded with moonlight. Jurek could be seen from a long distance off.

"Please, please," Lini muttered, without even knowing she was talking.

A sigh arose from the group as Jurek disappeared into the deep shadow cast by the building.

"All right, Otto," said Norbert, "you and me still have these triangles on."

Cutting the stitches of Norbert's insignia, Otto observed reflectively, "We need Jurek, but he doesn't need us."

"He feels solid to me. I think he meant it when he said he'd stick with us."

"But he doesn't *need* us. It would be better if he did."

2

Lini and Claire had moved off a short distance to relieve themselves. Now they were sitting together on a fallen tree, huddled close, hands thrust into opposite sleeves.

"You know what I was thinking about on the way?" Lini whispered. "My Joey. Maybe now I'm really going to see him."

Claire nodded.

"He'll be seven years old soon. He won't know me."

Claire said nothing. The year before it had been "He's six now", and the year before that "He's five – I haven't seen him for three whole years." Claire loved Lini dearly, and loved the two-year-old child Lini had described to her ten thousand times. She knew the address on the outskirts of Amsterdam where the child had been

placed, and she had pledged to adopt him if Lini did not survive
– but she had long since run out of any comments she could make
in reply to Lini's wistful, compulsive phrase, "Maybe now I'm
really going to see him."

"Ah, what a beautiful night!" Claire whispered after a few
moments. "There's something so pure and lovely about moonlight on snow."

"Sometime I hope you'll see Amsterdam with the canals
frozen and people skating and snow on the roofs. Like a Bruegel
painting."*

"It's so peaceful here – so peaceful," Claire murmured. "I could
sit here for ever." And then, with a burst of feeling: "These few
minutes without guards and dogs are worth so much to me that
if I have to die now, I don't care."

"Sure," Lini commented mockingly, "if you have to die now, you
don't care. My French romantic – what a little moonlight can do
for you! I wish it could inspire me the same way."

Claire laughed. "A lot of things inspire me – like that soup we
had."

"Wasn't it wonderful? My, it was wonderful! We haven't had
enough chance to talk about it."

"I'd forgotten what milk tastes like. If I ever get home, I'm going
to drink hot milk till I pee it."

"Those potatoes – real, honest potatoes. You realize we haven't
eaten good like that for two whole years?"

"Of course I realize! I wish I had some more of it now. I'm
hungry again."

"So why did you give me part of yours? You said you couldn't
eat any more."

"In my condition you mustn't eat much at a time. You can die
from filling up."

"Who says so?"

"Doctor Odette told me when I was getting over the typhus.
She said a normal meal, like people eat at home, would kill me."

"So I'm going to fall dead any minute, eh?"

33

"You're not as underweight as I am: your body can accept much more… Oh, look at that cloud! Like it was made of silver fleece… I wish I could lie on it and have it carry me to Paris while I ate potato soup every two hours. Then I'd walk down the Rue de Rivoli looking like a woman again."

"I wonder what the men think of us?"

"I'm sure they wished we looked human. Me, anyway. You don't look so bad."

"That Jurek's a handsome boy, isn't he?"

Andrey came over to them, flapping his arms to keep warm. He whispered to Claire in Russian. "It's not good for you to sit still in this cold. Either you should walk around or else begin massage."

"I guess you're right, thanks." She translated for Lini as she watched him walk off.

"Has you on his mind, hasn't he?" Lini observed a bit slyly. "Put your leg on my knees."

"He's very kind – they all are. We're so lucky to be with nice men like them. What would we have done alone?"

"Oh, my goodness, that's another word my Joseph could say. He would eat something he liked and say 'ni–i–ce'. Or when he was petting a pussycat. I haven't thought of that all these years, imagine!"

3

Some twenty minutes after he had left them, Jurek moved out from the factory shadow into the moonlight. He waved several times for them to come along and then stepped back into the darkness.

"Let's go together," Norbert suggested. "Claire, walk as fast as you can, eh? Lean on my arm, if you want."

"Wait," said Lini. "I'm the only one now with camp clothes. If we're seen, that's bad for all of you. You four go ahead, I'll come—"

"Nothing doing! Come along!"

Lini said nothing further, but her eyes were grateful.

The seventy-five yards of naked field was a nervous crossing. Claire pushed herself to the utmost, and her chest was heaving, her spindly thighs were trembling, when they arrived.

"Factory is empty," Jurek whispered.

They followed him around the side of the building through an open junkyard where boxes, shards of iron and broken machines and pieces of brick lay partially covered by snow. The front of the building faced a wide expanse of field, and there was the outline of a small road running out from its centre. There Jurek opened a door. They passed through a small vestibule and a second door, and found themselves in a large, bare room whose outlines they could discern quite easily because moonlight was streaming in through a wide window.

"I look everywhere," Jurek told them in normal tones. "First floor, too. Is no one here. Now I go to village. You wait."

"Where is it?" asked Otto.

Jurek gestured in the opposite direction from which they had come.

"I didn't see any houses."

"From upstairs I see in moonlight one house, maybe hundred fifty metres away. Village must begin there." He went out.

"How about a nip of cognac?" Otto asked.

Claire, who had already lain down on the floor, murmured, "No, thanks."

"I have a suggestion," Lini told him. "Cognac for the men, a piece of sugar for us."

"Why not? A good bargain." A bit ceremoniously Otto took out the paper bag and gave each of them two lumps.

"You're very kind," Claire murmured. She thrust both pieces into her mouth immediately.

"You'll do the same for me some day. Another slice of sausage?"

"We'd better save it," said Lini. She sat down by Claire and began massage.

The men sprawled on the floor, and the bottle circulated. "Only one swallow each, eh?" Otto remarked.

"Ah, how good that sugar was!" Claire said with a sigh. "Thank you again. What a wonderful day! We eat, we wash our faces… no dogs, no guards, no count. It's a dream."

With his nervous little chuckle Otto said, "Let's hope we don't wake up."

Lini reached into her jacket pocket, took out her two lumps of sugar and pressed them into Claire's hand.

"No," Claire protested.

"You gave me half your soup."

"And my shoes?"

"What are you talking about?"

"My birthday present. They must have cost you half your bread last week."

"Don't be a bookkeeper." Softly: "You need it, Claire. We must get you stronger."

Claire said nothing. This time she ate the sugar with delicate little nibbles, savouring each grain of sweetness.

"Won't be so bad if we can stay here," said Otto. "You notice there are double windows? Temperature must be fifteen degrees. We won't freeze."

"Depends if we can eat, if there are soldiers around," Norbert commented. "And I don't like it that we left tracks in the snow."

Andrey got up and walked to one side of the window so that he couldn't be seen from outside. The window was very wide, taking up a third of the wall space. Absently he began to hum.

"What's that?" Claire asked after a few moments.

He didn't answer.

"Got a bad ear, evidently," Lini whispered. She lay down by Claire's side. "I'm tired now. Massaging you is work. I have to rest a while."

"Of course. You remember that beautiful cloud?"

"Yes."

"I can see it before my eyes now."

"You look at the cloud. I'll look into the window of a delicatessen in Amsterdam. No, maybe I'll change that. A bakery with cakes."

4

It was an hour before Norbert, taking a turn at the window, announced Jurek's return. He came in rubbing his ears, a radiant smile on his face. "We have very good fortune," he announced with delight. "In the very first house I go is farmer – Karol his name. First he say nothing, he careful. He want see my Auschwitz tatto. When I tell him I fight with Polish partisans, he get more friendly, but ask questions, many. Then, when he believe me, he say he will help us every way he can. He is patriot."

There was a sigh in the room, as though all had been holding their breaths, and then a small tumult of rejoicing.

"You're wonderful," Lini cried. Norbert clapped Jurek on the shoulder. "None of us could have done it!"

"He will give us to eat," Jurek went on happily. "He is poor, but he will get from other farmers."

"But to stay in here is safe?" Andrey asked.

"Safe, yes! No Germans in village. Is very small village. No soldiers come since harvest."

Jurek went on to tell them that the farmer had imposed two conditions: they were not to light a fire, and they were never to go outside – only he, who could pass as a relative of Karol, would do so. It seemed there were some in the neighbourhood whose backbone Karol didn't trust. Escaped prisoners in a village invited reprisals. If they were seen, someone might report them out of fear to the Gestapo in Katowice. That was the only danger.

"So then we just stay here cosy till the Russians come!" Otto exclaimed blissfully. "Jurek, I award you the gold medal of... I don't know... something."

"I go back now to Karol," Jurek said. "His sister make something to eat for us."

"Another meal so soon?" Claire asked with enchantment. "We've moved from Auschwitz to paradise."

"Listen," said Norbert, "ask Karol if he has any clothes for Lini."

Jurek nodded.

"Something else," Lini suggested. "Can you bring some water from his house so we can wash?"

"Oh!" Claire exclaimed. "Do you think he might give us a piece of soap?"

"And maybe he has some blankets," Otto added.

Jurek burst out laughing. "Is only poor farmer, is not department store in Warsaw – but I ask, I see." He went out, leaving a hush behind him.

5

Not one of the five but was already thinking of home, of faces, of streets – and wondering if home, faces, streets, still were there. "Has Rostock been bombed?" Norbert wondered. "Will Joey be there?" Lini asked herself. "What if I get home safe and he..." She shut off the thought.

Out of the silence Claire spoke in Russian to Andrey, asking a question decisive for all of them: how long might it take for the Russian army to reach them? Andrey shrugged and answered that there was no telling. In the last months the advance had been rapid. They might be here in a few days, or they might be held where they were for weeks, or they might shift their attack to different sectors and not come this way for months.

Claire translated for the others. It was not the reply they wanted. Norbert asked, "Those guns we heard tonight – how far are they?"

"Twenty, twenty-five kilometres. But are German. Russians more far."

"Well, so we'll just keep house till they come," Lini stated cheerfully. "I'm happy!... Let's work on the other one, Claire."

Otto came over to them, sausage and knife in hand. "There's no need to save this now. How about some more?"

They accepted with thanks. He stood smiling, surveying them. "Why'd you girls get sent to Auschwitz? Let's get to know each other, what d'you say?"

"Let's hear about you first," Lini answered.

"Women are more interesting."

"There are more of you men."

"All right, short and sweet." He sat down cross-legged in front of them. "Shut your ears, Norbert. He knows all about me, and I know all about him. We're fed up with each other." He chuckled.

Cupping his ear, Andrey sat down beside Otto. Norbert, a bit away, was stretched out, hands behind his head.

"I'm from Vienna," Otto began. "My old man was a socialist, that's how I come to be sitting here right now. If he hadn't been, then who knows where I might—"

"You'd have been in Hitler's army," Norbert interrupted, "and probably dead or crippled by now. Would that have been better?"

"Who says better?" Otto snapped with annoyance. "You and me have been over all that. I'm just telling the facts, that's all. Don't interrupt... Well, do any of you remember the socialist revolt we had in '34?"*

"I don't," Claire murmured.

"I remember very well," Lini stated. "The government was turning fascist – the Social Democrats tried to stop it, no?"

"More or less like that. Anyway, I was smack in the centre of it. My family lived in the district where the Schutzbund – the Socialist Defence Force – had its main strength. Government troops surrounded us and started pounding with artillery. At that time I was..." He broke off. "How old do I look, girls?"

A reply was slow in coming. Lini felt he looked thirty-five, Claire would have guessed a few years younger, but both knew what camp life and a shaven head did to a prisoner's appearance. "About thirty?" Lini asked.

"Thirty!" Otto repeated in a small voice. "I'm twenty-four!" He erupted with bitterness: "The dogs stole seven years of my life. Christ, I'd like to get my hands on one Nazi, just one."

"Why only one?" Norbert enquired drily.

"So go on with Vienna," Lini said.

"Well... at the time of the fighting I was thirteen. My old man was the Schutzbund commander in our block of flats. I carried messages and ammunition – in the last day I was shooting, too. Well, they really gave us a tough time of it. My old man and a lot of others were sent to a concentration camp. After a year he was let out. In the mean time I'd become a hot socialist in the youth organization, thought I was a big fish, even made speeches. Another slice of roast beef, girls?"

"Just for Claire," Lini told him.

Claire started to protest, and Lini interrupted. "You'd do it for me if I was weaker than you – and we'd both do it for the men if they needed it. Why don't you stop this nonsense once and for all?"

"Is correct," said Andrey.

Otto handed Claire a slice of the sausage. "Take whatever you can get, that's my motto."

"Thank you. Please go on."

"Well, I skip to March '38, when Norbert's Germany took over my Austria—"

Norbert snapped up to a sitting position, and his voice was sharp. "It was Hitler's Germany took over Austria, not mine! Mine was in prison or dead or unable to speak out."

Otto laughed. "See, girls? All I have to do is press the right button and he lights up like an electric bulb."

"Please go on," Lini said, distressed.

"Well, the Gestapo came in to clean up Austria. I was seventeen, just falling in love for the first time, ha-ha. So…" He whistled and dusted off his hands. "When I opened my eyes, where was I? Me and my old man were in a brand-new health resort, Mauthausen. Hot and cold running lice, six-hour counts on your knees in the rain, all the trimmings. They beat my old man to death the first month. Mauthausen until '43, and then Auschwitz. From the time I was arrested until today I never saw a woman's face. Seven years! You don't mind if I stare at you both all day tomorrow, do you? I tried to be a gentleman this afternoon."

"Seven years!" Claire whispered. "How could you take it?"

With his quick, nervous chuckle, "Guess I'm tough."

"Tough wasn't enough," Norbert commented. "Luck, and a lot else."

"Norbert's the one who knows," Otto began – and then went rigid, as did all of them, at a clanking noise outside. They heard the outer door open with a creak of hinges. The clanking was repeated.

Norbert leapt up. "It *must* be Jurek!" He pulled open the inner door. Tension gave way to laughter. Jurek came in like an overloaded pedlar, carrying three stacked milk pails with one hand, a large wicker basket with the other and, on his back, a cardboard suitcase that had been tied with cord around his neck. As Norbert relieved him of the suitcase, he announced with a laugh, "I ask for everything like I was member family. In there is two blankets, clothes for Lini. Sister give clothes – nice Karol have very nice sister, too." Out of the top milk pail he lifted spoons, forks, a stack of soup plates, all of wood. He pulled a small chisel from his pocket. "To break ice in well. Factory has water well, I find later."

"Any soap?" Claire enquired eagerly.

"No soap, no towels, no salt, no milk – Germans take Karol last cow at harvest. But" – he opened the basket – "a little bit bread, and *plenty* hot cabbage and potatoes."

"Cabbage!" Lini exclaimed with rapture. "My God!"

"Is good man, Karol, no?" Jurek asked with pride.

"I wish we could thank him in person," Claire said fervently.

Andrey spoke in Russian, and Claire translated. It was a promise that when his comrades came, Karol would be repaid double for all he was doing.

Otto said, "Hey – did you think of asking for vodka?"

"Oh, he offer big bottle vodka, but I no take," Jurek replied airily. "*Didn't take it?*"

"I no like vodka, only French cognac."

"What's the matter with you?" Otto sputtered. "Are you—"

Jurek interrupted with a snort of laughter. "I make joke. Is no vodka."

For the third time since they had come together, the group exploded with laughter. It was a venting of mirth that had less to do with the jest than with their inner pressures.

"Well, now," Lini said when they had quieted, "let's eat while it's still hot."

"We get no more till tomorrow night," Jurek reminded them. "Is good we leave some for tomorrow, yes?"

Norbert said, "Lini, why don't you take charge? Divide it up for three meals."

"All right. Carry it over to the other side for me, will you? I can't see well enough."

The moon had been shifting, and now only the far end of the room had any radiance. They gathered there. Shortly all had a heaped soup plate of cabbage and potatoes, and a thick slice of home-made dark bread. "And there's enough for two meals more," Lini told them joyously.

Except for brief exclamations of pleasure, they ate in silence. They were utterly absorbed in the exquisite experience of foods they had not eaten for so long, in the satisfaction of being quit at last of the watery, foul-tasting nettle soup that had been their main meal of the day in Auschwitz. Cabbage, potatoes and tasty bread – it was a king's banquet. Of all of them, only Claire, by an effort of will, ate slowly. The others filled their mouths without pause, compelled by a need that was less one of acute hunger, since they had eaten well not many hours before, than one of the spirit. Each swabbed his plate clean with his last morsel of bread. "Ah," Otto exclaimed as he put his plate down, "St Karol! He will go straight to heaven."

Jurek said, "I could eat right now maybe ten more plates like this."

Andrey laughed. "Me, twenty."

They fell at once into a familiar prisoner pastime. "If you could have any dish you wanted for breakfast tomorrow," Lini asked Norbert, "what would it be?"

The answer was prompt. "Four ducks and four litres of beer."

There was a burst of laughter.

Otto: "For me, pot roast and dumplings."

Claire: "A great big cheese omelette."

Jurek: "A little pig, maybe six kilos, so I have little bit lunch, too."

More laughter.

Andrey: "Nice, fat goose."

Lini: "I can't decide between fresh Dutch herrings… and strawberries and sweet cream."

"Stuff the herrings with the strawberries," said Otto.

Claire set down her plate, which still was two thirds full. "All of you will be jealous of me later," she told them gaily. "See how much I still have to eat."

Lini: "I'm especially jealous. Your figure is so slender…"

Howls of laughter – Claire's the loudest.

"Now," said Jurek with a sigh, "I go find well, bring water."

"While you're doing that," Otto told him, "stop at the shop, will you, and buy me some cigars?"

Uproarious laughter!

"Oh my God," said Lini, "I'm weak. Don't anybody say another word."

Contentment in the room! A feeling of exquisite relaxation!

6

Moving cautiously in the darkness, Andrey sidled over to Claire. Norbert and Otto were dozing, lying together on one of the blankets. The two women had been resting also, but Andrey had seen Claire move and sit up. He whispered in Russian, "Claire – you wake up?"

"I wasn't asleep." She giggled a little, happily. "I'm eating again."

"Your feet hurt?"

"Like before, an ache."

"But not any worse?"

"No. But they're still icy cold. I wish I could put them in hot water for a few hours."

"That would be bad for them. The cool temperature in here is correct for your condition."

"How do you know all this?"

"Twice, before I was captured, my feet were frostbitten."

"What service were you in?"

"Medical. Ambulance attendant."

A moment of silence.

"Andrey, how is it you can hum a theme from Debussy so clearly that I recognize it? Are you a musician?"

He tried to answer matter-of-factly, but an inner sadness spilled over. "I was before the war. Now I don't know."

"Because you haven't been playing?"

"Not that. Until I was captured I did have the chance to practise when I was off duty. But I've lost most of the hearing in my right ear. From concussion... my ambulance struck a mine. To be a first-class musician is never easy. But if you're handicapped... I don't know if I'll be able to hear music in a balanced way any more, or if I can learn to compensate."

"When you get home, perhaps with medical help?..."

"Perhaps."

Silence.

"Claire, you like classical music, eh?"

"Oh, yes! Chamber music especially. What's your instrument?"

"The cello."

"Were you in an orchestra?"

"No. I was a student at the conservatory in Kiev." Wryly: "I was very promising, they said. When the war came, I was preparing my first public concert."

"You never gave it?"

"No."

Again a moment of silence.

"How old are you, Andrey?"

"Twenty-five... I suppose I look much older?"

"A little. All of us must."

"And you?"

"Twenty-six."

Softly: "You have such wonderful eyes, Claire. They remind me of the blue eyes of some of our Russian girls."

Claire laughed. "You don't know how French I am."

"But your grandfather makes you part Russian, I insist," he said jestingly. "Ah, it's wonderful that you speak Russian. In my work commando, in my block, there was no one – men from every other country. I know twenty words of ten languages now, even Greek." He laughed drily.

"Do I have much of an accent?"

"Very little. Is your Polish good, too?"

"No. I get along, that's all. I concentrated on German and Russian because I was preparing to be a translator."

"To translate books?"

"Yes. I thought it would be an interesting way to earn a living."

"Have you translated some Russian books?" he asked eagerly.

"No, I never worked professionally. I married and then the war came."

After a moment's hesitation: "And your husband?"

Softly, with no emotion breaking through: "He's dead. I never saw him after we got to Auschwitz."

The inner door opened noisily as Jurek came in with the last of the three pails of water.

"Hey," Otto said, rousing, "did you get my cigars?"

"Excuse me, sir, I forgot."

"Ha-ha."

"Time for the count?" Lini asked.

The room exploded with laughter – a laughter that was harsh, joyless, bitter and private to these six. More dreadful than almost anything else in camp life had been the dawn and dusk counts when all prisoners, in rigid lines before their blocks, had been forced to stand at attention or kneel with arms upraised for two and three and four hours in whatever weather, with the whip and the club waiting for those who fell. Their laughter didn't last long. When it stopped, there was sour anger in the room, and a rawness of nerves, and the clear air was filled with odours that each of them could smell: of the fetid blocks in which they had lived, of their own bodies unwashed week after week, of engorged lice crushed between fingernails, of human flesh burning day and night in the crematoria. Lini began to weep. "Oh, I'm so sorry I said that. Let's not talk of the camp any more – not any more."

"Shhh!" Claire said, putting an arm around her. "Friends... dear, good friends... I have a proposal. Our first night of freedom, let's forget the camp with music. Andrey just told me he's a musician. Let's ask him to sing something beautiful for us. Let's go to sleep with music."

"Very good," said Otto. "How about 'The Blue Danube'?"*

"Ah, no. All of us can sing that. Some melody from Beethoven or Tchaikovsky.* You'll do it, Andrey?"

"With pleasure," he answered in Russian. "But something simple, not Beethoven."

"You decide... He'll do it, friends."

They settled themselves for sleep, Lini and Claire with one of the blankets wrapped around them, the four men lying on the other blanket.

"Tell them," Andrey said in Russian, "that I will sing something written by the Czech composer Dvořák. In the army I carried my cello with me. Often I would play for wounded soldiers. This piece they asked for again and again. It is called 'Songs My Mother Taught Me'.* It is short, full of lovely sentiment."

She translated.

"And they should forgive my poor voice."

"Never mind."

They lay on the stone floor of this abandoned factory savouring their first night of freedom as Andrey half hummed, half sang. The fingers of his left hand played the notes on his chest without his being aware of it. They listened, and, except for Claire, drifted into sleep before he had finished.

"Thank you so much," she said when he was quiet. "Goodnight, Andrey. I need to sleep now."

"I'm so happy, I don't know if I'll be able to sleep." With a low laugh, "How is it I can see your eyes in the dark?"

"You can't. They're shut."

"Strange. I still see them."

"You're very flattering."

"I didn't hear you."

"I said that you're very flattering."

"It isn't flattery."

She laughed. "That's one thing a Frenchwoman always knows. But I like it. Goodnight."

"Goodnight, Claire."

Chapter 3

Between Heaven and Earth

I

At dawn, emerging from sleep, Otto waited for the morning shout from his foul-mouthed block leader and for the beat of his club on the wall in a warning to laggards: "*Up for the count, you sons of whores! Get your stinking pig asses outside quick!*" When the cry did not come, he opened his eyes in surprise – and then, fully aware at once, felt such bursting happiness that he could not contain it. He sat up, gazed at the others with radiant eyes and a wild grin, and suddenly began to yell at the top of his voice, "*Get up, you filth! Outside for the count! Quick! Quick!*"

If Otto had been a more sensitive man, he would have regretted his burlesque immediately. The five figures burst from their slumber with the sighing groans, the grimaces of tension, the drugged, forced movements that he had seen for so many years. They were on their feet before his guffaws brought their response to a halt. No answering concert of laughter came from them as he had expected. In that moment all hated him, and he saw it in their eyes and frozen faces, and his own laughter died. "A joke," he muttered.

There was a long silence that finally was broken by Lini. "Please," she said gently, "let's not make jokes like that any more. I did it last night, too. It's a mistake. We've all suffered too much."

"Sure," Otto muttered. "I'm sorry. I didn't think…"

Norbert tapped his arm in a friendly way and said, "Easy does it."

"Oh, look!" Claire cried with rapture. She was pointing to the window. "No blocks, no fence, no watchtowers! Look how beautiful it is!"

They crowded in front of the window. The dawn was sunless, the sky a grey, slate colour, similar in its oppressive, wintry aspect to many other mornings they had known – but now, for them, something wondrous. From the door of the factory a small road ran into the distance between flat, snow-covered fields. As far as the eye could see in every direction, there were no houses or people, and no tracks marred the wide expanse of snow. In the far, far distance, there was a thick wood. They stared avidly at the peaceful scene, their eyes gleaming, each feeling his freedom with a keenness that had not been possible in the darkness of the previous night. Claire and Lini turned to each other with radiant smiles. Spontaneously they embraced. "My God," Lini whispered, "what a long road from Toulouse!"

"Did you ever see anything so lovely?" Claire murmured with enchantment. "If I have to die now, I don't care. Not after this sight."

Lini grinned. "That's twice in twenty-four hours you've been ready to die."

"Ah, friends, friends," Claire exclaimed joyously, without taking her eyes from the view outside, "only four days ago, when we woke up in the morning, we were numbers… slaves… dirt. Now each one of us has his own character again, his own pride, his own humanity. Oh, what the word 'freedom' means! I feel as though I'll jump out of my skin with happiness."

Lini suddenly gestured for Claire to turn around. Norbert was standing before the window oblivious of everyone and of the fact that tears were slipping down his cheeks. The other men, noticing, walked away from the window to allow him his privacy. Claire followed, but Lini did not. She moved over to him, waited a moment, then spoke softly. "Norbert?" She touched his arm, "Norbert?" He turned, came to himself, felt the tears on his cheeks and wiped them away.

"Were you in a long time?"

He nodded. She could see him swallow.

"How long?"

"Arrested in '33."

"Twelve years? My God!"

"I never believed I'd be standing free like this," he muttered. "I saw my friends go one by one. I hoped, but I never believed it."

She put her hand on his arm. "Here we are, though."

"Yes." His body slumped, and the strong, controlled look on his face gave way to one that was sombre and tired and much softer. "I feel," he said, "like a man who has…" – he gestured aimlessly – "has climbed the steepest mountain in the world, let's say… and once on top… begins to know for the first time what it cost him to get there. I feel… worn out. Not in my body, but in my head and my heart."

Lini's hand still was on his arm. "Of course," she murmured, "twelve years, my God! But you'll come back to yourself. You must be a very strong man, or you wouldn't have come through." And then, because she knew too keenly herself what it felt like to be worn out in heart and mind, she sought for a way to break his mood. "Pay attention, everybody," she called loudly. "We can't go outside, so we better decide what corner of this building is the women's latrine. And we better do it right this minute, or I'm going to disgrace myself: my bladder's bursting."

Laughter, and the faint smile she hoped for from Norbert!

"This was a factory – why wouldn't it have lavatories?" Otto asked. "Let's look for 'em. I haven't seen a real lavatory for seven years."

Claire giggled. "For years he hasn't seen a woman's face or a lavatory. Lini, what'll we do if he looks at the lavatory all day instead of at us?"

"Ha-ha. I wouldn't look at it all day, but if the place was warm, I might sit on it all day for the experience."

They opened the door at the rear of the room to find themselves in the odd emptiness of a factory that had been stripped of every machine, every belt, every wire. Only a red dust over the floor, and holes in the concrete where machines had been bolted down, gave any sign of its former usage.

"Looks like brick dust," Norbert commented.

"Is so," Jurek told them. "Was brick factory. Germans take everything." He pointed towards a door. "Through that door is stair to first floor. A-ha!" He indicated a corner of the room, where two enclosed cubicles broke the line of the wall. "Lavatories there, I think."

"We're like the crew of Columbus discovering America," Claire remarked with a giggle as they crossed the floor. Then she pointed. "I see the signs – for women, for men."

"Ah, yes," Jurek said to her in Polish. "I forgot you speak my language."

"Not very well, really. I just picked up some from my grandmother."

Otto pulled open the door of the women's lavatory and planted himself in front of it. "Why, it *is* more beautiful than a woman. Look how it's shaped. No woman—"

"Out of the way, please," said Lini.

Otto didn't move. "I'm a lover of beauty. Let me enjoy it a moment."

Lini tried to shove him aside, but he stayed rooted. "Otto, I'm bursting."

"For the sake of the Third Reich, you must learn to discipline your bladder."

"Pfui!" she retorted with a snort of laughter, and quickly entered the other cubicle.

Otto offered his arm to Claire. "Madame – can I escort you to the door of America?"

2

They sat in a circle, the blankets over their shoulders, while Lini portioned out their breakfast. Andrey, by Claire's side, asked softly in Russian, "How are the feet this morning?"

"Better, I think. I can move my toes. I couldn't last night."

"Ah, good. May I see how they feel?"

"Of course."

He slipped his fingers down into the hay boot of each foot in turn. "Still cold, but not as icy as yesterday." He smiled, and a glow came to his dark-brown eyes. "Yesterday I was a little afraid of gangrene. Now there's no worry. But the massage has to continue. And move your toes often."

"Gangrene? That would have finished me, wouldn't it?"

"In these circumstances, yes."

"That would've been a stupid end after living through Auschwitz."

"Hey," said Otto with a slight undertone of resentment, "why don't you two talk German so we can all understand?"

"No secret," Claire told him with a smile, "just about my feet. It's so much easier for Andrey to speak Russian."

Lini began to hand out the soup plates. Breakfast offered a third less of the cabbage and potatoes than the night before – and now cold, and only half a piece of bread each – but their mouths watered at the sight of their plates, and they felt blessed. Breakfast in Auschwitz had been herb coffee or tea, and a chunk of sour, ill-tasting bread – provided they had saved any bread from their issue of the previous evening. This time there was not quite so much haste to their eating, and bits of conversation accompanied it.

"Hey, look what I found!" Otto extended his fork with half a potato on it. "A nice piece of roast pork."

Lini: "I cooked it especially for you."

On its way to his mouth a piece of the potato dropped to the floor. Otto picked it up, brushed it off and popped it into his mouth. There was no one among them that would not have done the same.

"Good, no?" Jurek exclaimed. He patted his belly. "Not so empty any more."

"We're eating like block leaders and capos now," said Norbert with amusement.

Otto: "Isn't it the truth? Hey, Claire" – he handed her two pieces of sugar. "Your dessert."

"Thank you, Otto. You're very nice." She hesitated a moment, then spoke from her heart. "Without you men we would have been lost. Or with different men it might have been… bad for us. But you're such good comrades to us…well, just understand that we appreciate it with all our hearts."

"Think nothing of it… we're just four gentlemen from Auschwitz," said Otto. He jumped up. "No: the four musketeers – my favourite book when I was a kid." He began a duel in pantomime. "We defend ladies from all dangers." He slashed the air frenetically. "One dead, two dead, three dead" – slash, a gruesome gargle. "Now I'm dead." He flopped down.

Laughter and applause. Pleased, Otto picked up his plate and popped some cabbage into his mouth.

Andrey said to Claire in Russian, "You have a lovely smile. Before Auschwitz I think you must have been a beautiful woman."

Rather sombrely she replied, "Thank you, Andrey. When you say something like that, it helps me feel a little like a woman again."

"But what else do you feel like?" he asked with surprise.

"Something neuter."

"But why?"

She answered with a candour that once would have been impossible with a strange man. But life in Auschwitz had been reduced to a plane so naked and elemental that reticence had been shorn from the personality of prisoners like the hair from their heads. "My body's a skeleton – I haven't menstruated for two years; I don't have a woman's hair or normal breasts."

"How is it I regard you as very much a woman?"

"Perhaps because you haven't seen women for so long. Or" – with a sly look – "maybe you can't help being gallant with any woman."

"Neither," he replied earnestly. "I've only been a prisoner seven months. Besides, every day my commando would march past the women's camp in Birkenau, so I would see women. But in spite of your clothes and your physical state, you're very feminine. Your eyes, your lips, your voice… your gestures, your whole personality – so very feminine."

Claire smiled at him, and was more grateful than he could have known. "That's lovely to hear. Thank you, Andrey. Oh!" She turned abruptly and spoke in German. "Jurek, do you think you could bring us a mirror?"

"I will ask."

"Did you men get a chance to see yourselves? We didn't – except a few times, when the light was right, in a window pane. But you couldn't really see."

It turned out that the men also had not seen themselves for the years of their imprisonment. Norbert said, "Once in Buchenwald I got hold of a tiny piece of mirror, but all I could see was part of my nose or a part of my mouth. It was worse than nothing."

"Are you sure you want to see yourself?" Lini asked Claire with a laugh. "I'm not."

"I'm gaining weight by the minute on this good food," Claire replied happily. "By tomorrow I'll be looking normal."

"Yah, yah!" Gathering the plates of the others Lini said, "You should have seen Claire before Auschwitz – not plain Dutch like me, but stunning, an elegant French beauty. Well, gentlemen, as soon as I wash these plates, you will kindly take a small walk so the girls around here can bathe. After that I'll be able to wear the clothes Jurek got at the Karol department store. Oh my goodness, I haven't even looked at them!" She dropped the plates with a clatter, opened the suitcase and began to squeal with delight as she pulled out successive garments – blue wool skirt, flannel petticoat, high-necked peasant blouse, a heavy wool sweater. "My God – look, look!" she kept exclaiming. "I'll be a queen." The garments were patched and far from new, but her pleasure in them was not diminished. "So now go out, eh?" she said to the men. She was fitting the skirt to her waist.

Norbert said, "Lini, you've got all day to bathe, and the water won't get any colder by waiting. We don't know a thing about you girls."

"We've got all day to talk, too. I want to get out of these clothes and put Auschwitz behind me."

"Let's have a vote," Otto suggested. "What should Lini do first – tell us about herself or wash? All in favour of the first?"

The four men, grinning in unison, raised their hands.

"Majority decision. Sit down, Lini. This is a democracy."

"Claire, you know what?" Lini said. "This skirt is certainly too big in the waist. What'll I do?"

"Maybe Jurek can get some safety pins."

"Ah, I forget. Karol sister ask me how is your shape." His smile flashed. "She is little bit fatter than you. So" – he took several safety pins from a pocket – "she give me these."

"Bless Karol's sister! Now, men, outside, eh?"

"Majority decision," Otto repeated with a grin. "Where were you born, when did you learn to read, what was the name of the first boy you kissed, et cetera?"

"Please, Lini," Norbert said quietly. "We don't want to stay strangers."

"How stubborn you men are!" She sat down. "Claire, give me a leg, and I'll put the time to good use. So, where do I begin? Well, I was born in Amsterdam. I had a very nice mother – she died just before the war, I'm glad of that – and two older brothers who live in Canada… I don't know what's happened to them, prob- ably they're in the Canadian army… and I had a father who was narrow-minded, very religious and an idiot…"

She paused briefly.

"I imagine he's dead now – he wouldn't leave Amsterdam. Anyway, he had a small butcher shop. I went to elementary school only, and then I worked in a chocolate factory. But I studied at night to become a secretary – and I did, finally. After that, I worked as a typist in an office. In 1936 I got married. Two years later we had a boy, Joseph. So that's the preliminaries."

Lini's manner of speaking, which until now had been rapid and casual, changed abruptly. She spoke more slowly, and emotion began to seep into her tone, despite her obvious effort to be controlled. "Now I'll go to the day that started me towards Auschwitz. It was almost five years ago, May the 9th."

"Why that day?" Norbert asked.

"The Germans invaded Belgium, France and Holland." She paused for a moment and then said wryly, "Not exactly like remembering a birthday or a wedding anniversary, is it? The minute it started, my husband and I knew we had to run – we'd talked it over many times before. We were both Jewish, and we understood very well what fascism meant. Some Jews, like my stupid father, had illusions. But my husband, Alex, had been a member of an anti-Nazi organization. He was a marked man, in fact, because he used to make speeches at meetings. In fact, he once was beaten up by some Dutch fascists who told him that next time it would be curtains."

"What work did your husband do?" Norbert asked.

"He was a teacher in a grammar school. He was a good deal older than me, fifteen years."

"And how old are you now?"

"Twenty-nine. At that time our boy was only two. We'd made preparations beforehand, naturally. We left him with some Christian friends." She paused and tried to blink away sudden tears. "You don't know what a sweet child he is. He'll be almost seven now – he won't know me. I don't even know if he's alive."

"Why shouldn't he be?" Norbert asked heartily. "Of course he is!"

"Who knows what's happened in these years?" She brushed at her eyes. "So, my husband and I left Holland on bicycles. We went from Amsterdam across Belgium to Paris. Sometimes we were quite near fighting, and we had to go all different directions. We were two weeks on the road, we got to Paris half dead."

"How did you cross borders?" Otto asked.

"At night, paying a guide. My husband's French was good – he studied in France – so he could manage things well. We stayed in Paris with some friends of his until the French armies began to fall apart – and then, like everybody else, we ran south. We stopped at Toulouse, where Alex had another friend. He helped us get refugee papers – without them we couldn't have had food cards. So we stayed there until France surrendered. At that time Toulouse was safe for us, because it wasn't in the part occupied by the Nazis, but Alex felt it wouldn't be safe for long. Besides, he wanted to get to England and join the British army." Lini paused in her narrative to adjust Claire's leg on her lap. "Am I making this too long?"

"No, no," Norbert told her eagerly. "You don't realize – there's so much Otto and I don't know about what happened in the war. We'd like to hear everything. You wanted to go to England. What happened?"

"We went down to the Spanish border at Perpignan. We sold our bicycles. Alex found a guide who would lead us at night past the border guards. He took our money and led us directly to a Spanish patrol. We were in jail for a week, then they deported us back to France. So that ended it for England. We got back to Toulouse with hardly a franc. But there were other refugees there, German Jews mostly, and Alex earned a little money teaching French to them."

"And how did the French people treat you?" Norbert asked.

"Mostly very well. Of course, they had their fascists, too. So, more than a year passed. Then, in December '42, the Germans took over unoccupied France." Lini stopped massaging Claire's leg. A stiffness came into her posture – her lips tightened, her voice became small. "There was nothing we could do, nowhere to run, no place for Jews like us to hide. It was awful waiting to be arrested. After three weeks we were. That was how I met Claire. They put me in a cell with her, thank God. But Alex..." She stopped, then gestured with her head for Claire to tell them.

"They shot Alex," Claire said. "They got his record from Holland and shot him."

"My German brothers!" Norbert exclaimed in a burst of passion. "For twelve years I've kept asking myself how this racist insanity could grow in a people like mine. I know all the answers to it – political, economic, historical. Believe me, to be in Dachau in the early years was to be with many educated men, the best of Germany – professors, scholars, writers, men who *knew* things. Ten thousand hours I listened to them talk, like going to a university for a working man like me. But still, even now, even though I know all the answers, I ask myself: how was it possible?"

They were silent suddenly, because all of them had pondered this endlessly in the mad abattoir of Auschwitz. Andrey told Claire in Russian that he had missed some of what Norbert said because he had spoken so quickly. Claire repeated the gist of it to him, and he nodded approvingly. Presently Lini went on in her small, tight voice. "So now you know all about me. From Toulouse they sent me to Drancy, where they collected French Jews for deportation, and from there I was shipped to Auschwitz in March '43." She paused, and her wide, generous mouth twisted in a wry smile. "Well, that's the story."

They were quiet for a few moments. Abruptly Lini said, "No, that isn't the *whole* story! I need to tell you about this one." She glanced at Claire. Her face had softened in the instant, and her eyes began to glow as she talked. "In the Toulouse jail you could starve as badly as in Auschwitz. But this one got packages. She didn't know me – I was a foreigner – but from the first minute she shared everything with me."

"And what have you done for me?" Claire asked fondly.

Ignoring her, Lini said with intense feeling, "When my husband was shot, and I wanted to beat my brains out against the wall, there was Claire – forcing me to think of my child, holding me when I cried, staying awake with me when I couldn't sleep… my God, you don't know what a wonderful heart she has! Just think: she was in Auschwitz as an interpreter – I was still in Birkenau* in a field commando. How long would I have lasted working in swamp water? Claire kept begging the Gestapo officer she worked for to put me in the office as a typist. She made such a nuisance of herself that one day he said, 'I have to make a choice: either take your friend out of Birkenau or send you back there. Otherwise you won't shut up about her, will you?' And Claire said, 'No, sir, I can't.' Those were the exact words, he told me so himself later – he couldn't help admiring her, the bastard. But Claire was too useful to him, so I got out of Birkenau. Otherwise I'd have been ashes long ago. That's the kind of girl Claire is."

Smiling, Claire said, "And you know, Lini never did a thing for me in return. A few little things maybe – such as watching for every French transport that came to Birkenau. In the first week I got there, she had a food pan for me, a slip, a sweater – all bought on the black market by selling her bread. And when I had typhus, with that high fever and terrible thirst it brings, who starved herself to bring me her soup day after day?"

"Yes," Norbert said emphatically, "you're both alive because of each other. I've seen it a thousand times. Let me tell you something." His face had become very animated, and his voice began to resound. "In Dachau, in Majdanek, in Auschwitz, I saw men become wild beasts – stealing from each other, informing, caring for nothing except themselves. It must have been the same among you women."

"Of course," said Lini. "And the worst were those who became block leaders and capos – clubbing other prisoners, stealing their food—"

"Yes," Norbert interrupted, "but that isn't what I'm talking about. All human beings want to survive. In terrible conditions many go to pieces – they give up and die, or they stay alive by becoming animals. Yet others don't! That's what kept me going for twelve years – the real guts, and the real nobility and kindness I saw in some men. They did everything to stay alive, but certain things they wouldn't do – and what they wouldn't do kept them men. In Majdanek I was quite good pals with a highly educated man from Hungary, a book publisher. He said to me once something like this: 'In many people loyalty to an ideal, or to a friend, is so strong that it becomes more important than just keeping yourself alive. It's such feelings that make people really human,' he said. That's why Claire didn't let you down, Lini, and why you didn't let her down. And it's why you're both still alive!"

"Ah, look," Claire said softly. "It's beginning to snow. How beautiful!"

"Is very good luck for us," Jurek pointed out instantly. "It will hide our foot tracks from woods."

"Snug as bugs in a rug we are!" Otto exclaimed with satisfaction. "The four musketeers and their ladies!" He jumped up and began humming 'The Blue Danube'. "C'mon," he said to Lini, holding out his hands, "I haven't danced with a lady for at least a week or two."

Smiling, Lini joined him. Andrey began to sing the tune. Presently all were singing and humming while Otto and Lini waltzed gaily and clumsily around the room.

3

It took a bit of discussion before Lini and Claire decided on the best technique of bathing. The problems were formidable: a cold room, a single bucket of cold water, no soap, no washcloth, no towel. Yet, to clean their bodies as best they could was a moral, as well as a physical, imperative. Life in Auschwitz had been a constant struggle against typhus-carrying lice, with only a two-minute shower bath once a month. As they had yearned daily for food, so they had yearned to be clean.

They decided that Claire's slip would be the washcloth and Lini's the towel. They took off their clothes, and each quickly enveloped herself in one of the blankets. "Let's do like a sponge bath when someone is sick," Lini suggested. "Wash an arm, dry it, cover it up – then the other arm, and so on." They were proceeding in this way, Lini ministering to Claire first.

"The fine art of bathing!" Claire murmured with chattering teeth. "The first time I see a bathtub I'll kiss it."

"This rubbing gets the dirt off pretty well. Want me to do your head, too?"

"Oh, please. If there are any lice eggs, don't tell me."

"So take off your kerchief – I'm not being paid for that."

Claire combined a chuckle and a shiver.

"My, how fast your hair is growing!"

With delight: "Really?"

"At least I think so. Without a magnifying glass I can't be sure."

"*Salope!** I thought you meant it."

"What's that word?"

"Something nasty." With longing: "Won't it be wonderful to have hair again? To be a woman again?"

"You're a woman to Andrey. He keeps looking at you that way. Do you like him?"

"Very much."

"He has nice eyes. I imagine he's not bad-looking when he's eating normally. Since he's a musician, I'm sure he has wavy, romantic hair. What will you do when he wants to make love?"

"Are you joking?"

"No."

"You must be. What man would want *me*?"

"*Chérie,** you're an idiot. You may be skin and bones, but you're a woman. These men have been aching for a long time. If we stay together a few more days, don't you realize they'll start asking?"

"I just hadn't thought about it. But it won't do them any good with me. I couldn't respond – I'm dead that way. What about you?"

Lini laughed. "Let's see if I'm asked, and by who."

"You have feelings already?"

"I should say!"

"Would you worry about getting pregnant?"

"After what we've been through? Certainly not! Anyway, I haven't menstruated."

"Which of the men is it?"

"Guess."

"Jurek's the handsomest. He's as good-looking as a movie actor."

"Isn't he, though? No, not him, and not your Andrey. Let me do your back now."

"Then it's Norbert. You like him a lot?"

"I really do. He's the sort of man I've always been drawn to – quiet and strong. How'd you know it wasn't Otto?"

"Because I don't like him as much as the others. I don't quite know why, yet."

"I do – he's a bit foxy. You remember yesterday, when Norbert asked if he had any food? Did you notice?"

"Yes. Still he's been generous with the sugar."

"I'll tell you something. I woke up last night. Even in the dark I could tell he was eating sugar and finishing off the cognac."

"Oh?... Well, they were his in the first place. He's been in seven years. That does something to a man."

"Sometimes seven days does it and seven years doesn't... All right, my sweet. You're as clean as I can get you this morning."

"Find any eggs?"

"No. You want to put on your clothes before you do me?"

"Thanks, yes."

"Are you freezing?"

"Strangely enough I feel warmer now. The cold water and the rubbing must have made my blood circulate. Lini..."

"Yes?"

"Something worries me about you and Norbert."

"What?"

"It's a situation of four men and one woman. Or maybe only three men, because Andrey looks worn out, too. What's going to happen if you and Norbert become lovers?"

"Why should anything happen?"

"How do you think the others will feel?"

"Unlucky, I guess."

"It would be awful if that spoiled the way we're getting on together."

"I don't see why it should. If these were different men, it might. I was wondering when we went to sleep if I'd feel hands on me in the middle of the night. But it's clear they're decent. There's been no dirty talk – they don't even do any swearing in front of us."

"I've noticed that."

"Anyway, if Norbert asks me, I certainly won't say no." She paused for a second, and there was a catch in her voice when she went on. "I'm starved to have a man I like put his arms around me. I can't understand why you don't need it, too."

"I told you."

"I don't mean with your body, I mean with your feelings. I'm not burning up with sex either. But I need a man wanting me. Not any man, of course: someone I feel for. My heart needs it after all this time. Doesn't yours?"

"Not yet. A man would be too much for me right now. I haven't come that far back to life. I just want to eat and sleep and feel happy we're free… well, are you ready to have the dirt taken off you?"

"Yes," Lini answered. And then, in an eruption of anguished rage, "Scrub Auschwitz out of my heart, too, if you can!" She began to weep. "My God, Alex and I were so good together. He was all I wanted in a man. We had such a fine life with our little boy! Why did this have to happen to us?"

4

For a moment after Lini appeared in her new clothes, there was stunned silence among the men. Upon occasion during their imprisonment they had seen female guards in uniform, but none had seen a woman in normal garments. The high-necked, peasant blouse, the wide skirt, were very feminine, and even the kerchief seemed normal to Lini's apparel instead of the stigma of a shorn head. "Bravo!" Otto cried after a few moments, and began to applaud. Jurek and Andrey did the same. Norbert just stood gazing at Lini with a glow in his eyes. It was a reaction that touched both women deeply.

Watching them, Claire suddenly said to herself with absolute astonishment, "Why – I'm jealous!" An instant later she understood why. The clothes had changed Lini from fellow prisoner to woman – an excessively thin one, it was true, but nonetheless feminine, and magnetically attractive to these deprived men. It was this she was envious of – she with her boy's clothes, her emaciated body, her inert feelings.

Lini's smile and eyes showed how pleased she was, and Claire noted that her glance went to Norbert. Then she held out the bundle of camp clothes she was carrying. "Will you have Karol burn these damn things?"

"Why burn them?" asked Otto, snatching the bundle. He tossed it in the air, then jumped and hit it with his head. "We can use it to play football."

"On guard!" Jurek shouted. He manoeuvred the bundle from side to side in imitation of a soccer player, then gave it a kick. "Goal!"

"No goal – offside!"

While the others grinned, the two kicked the bundle back and forth – until the sleeves became untied and the striped dress and jacket unravelled and lay on the floor as an ugly reminder of what they had endured. Their laughter ended. Quietly Jurek picked up the garments. He took his cap from his pocket. "Is time we burn these too, no?"

Andrey, in a sudden movement, snatched his own cap from his head. "What is matter us? Is crazy still wear." He tossed the cap to Jurek with a grimace of disgust.

"We certainly aren't keeping our wits about us," Norbert muttered.

"I knew I was wearing mine," Otto told them. "Just wanted to keep my head warm. But I suppose it is better to get rid of 'em."

"Well, girls, have a nice bath?" Norbert asked, addressing Lini.

"Lovely. By the way, the water pipe in our lavatory is frozen. Now that we've dirtied the water in our bathtub, would you mind carrying it to our lavatory? The pail's heavy for us."

"Of course. Our pipe's frozen, too."

"Girls," said Otto, "there are about four more slices of sausage left. You hungry?"

"Just for Claire," Lini told him.

Otto took out his knife. "Aren't we a cosy family? First you bathe, then it's our turn... we eat three fine meals a day... we're out of the cold... away from the war... such little bugs snug in a rug. Madame... have you ever tasted our Polish ham? Famous even in Vienna before the war."

"Thank you, Otto," Claire said. "*I* feel as though we're a family, too – a wonderful family."

"*Sh!*" Jurek said. "Guns!"

They were quiet. Andrey cupped his ear.

"Rifles?" asked Norbert, pausing with the pail in his hand.

"Big guns."

They continued to listen.

"Mistake, I guess," Jurek murmured.

"How could you hear guns?" asked Otto. "We're on a desert island surrounded by water. Look at the palm trees. We're having baked coconut for dinner."

"*I* just heard them," Norbert said. "Like a roll of thunder far away."

Claire nodded. "I did, too." She turned to Andrey. "Does that mean the Russians are coming closer?"

He shrugged. "Is too far tell. Maybe only wind blow this way."

"Oh!" she exclaimed fervently, "it will be so good when they come closer. I want to *hear* their guns."

Andrey spoke quietly in Russian. "I have heard war close. There is not one sound in it that's good."

"I didn't mean it that way."

"I know you didn't. I spoke out of my own thoughts."

5

The snow was still falling, although lightly, and the view through the window was serene and lovely. The men had bathed – Lini had given Claire's legs a lengthy massage, and now Claire was sleeping. The underclothes of both the men and the women hung drying from the wide window ledge as might the family wash in a tenement. The guns, no longer heard, were out of memory. With the hunger for normality of those who have lived abnormally, the four men were listening to Lini talk about her child. Lini's voice had become rich and warm – little smiles flirted over her lips as she talked, and it was obvious that the boy was moving before her mind's eye as vividly as in life.

"I remember one of the last things I saw him do: he discovered himself in a big mirror we had on a cupboard door. He put his face close to it, then he moved away, then he got down on his knees to stare at it – and he kept looking *so* surprised. Finally, he tried to open the door to see where the other child was." She laughed softly. The men smiled.

"That same afternoon he was sitting in a corner of my bedroom pulling a small stool towards him and pushing it away, and babbling to himself. By accident he pulled it towards him a little too hard and it hit his head. He pushed it away very angrily, looked at me, pointed to his head and slapped the stool." She chuckled and sighed. "At that age a little one is so dear in everything he does. He loved to crawl upstairs and come down by bumping his little bottom from step to step. And he loved to go under things – under tables, my husband's desk, his own crib. Oh, I could talk about him for hours!"

"Talk, talk," said Norbert. His eyes were fixed on her – he was smiling with a tenderness that she found touching.

"You're not bored?" she asked happily, and thought to herself that Norbert looked altogether different from the man she had met twenty-four hours before. His strong, bony face had lost its tension.

"Bored? Of course not. Who doesn't like children? Everyone does. It's wonderful to hear you."

"Does a kid speak at that age?" Otto asked. "I forget."

"Oh yes! Not sentences, just words. But they understand an enormous amount, practically everything you tell them. That was something wonderful to me – the way a child gets to understand language. For instance, I would say to him, 'Joey, do you want your bath now?' He would answer, 'Uh, ba.' That meant, 'Yes, bath.' And then, if I made no move to take him to the bathroom, he would grab my hand and ask 'Ba-ba?' All children love to be bathed."

"Ba-ba," Norbert repeated with a smile. "What other words did he know? Mama and Papa, I suppose?"

"Yes, but he said them in a funny way of his own. Let's see… I have to translate from the Dutch… it was something like this: 'Mahnny' and 'Pa-ee'… And like all children of that age he used the same word for a lot of things. He said 'moh' for milk and water, 'dee-dee' for his pee-pee and the other, and 'mum-mum' for all foods." She began to laugh. "And the way he said 'kitty' – it was 'kit-li-lilli'. Why he made such a big word out of it I never understood. Oh, and one very precious word he had: 'Ahwanee' – meaning 'I want it'."

Lini's laughter cut off as the sharp barking of a dog came into the room from not far off.

"Away from window!" Andrey snapped, and all, on hands and knees, scattered to both sides.

The barking was continuous, the yap of a large dog.

"Let's hide upstairs," Lini cried in terror.

"Wait!" said Jurek. "I hear boy." Quickly he went at a crouch to one side of the window. The barking continued. Jurek's figure relaxed. "Is nothing. Is two boys throwing snowball."

"But if they come in here and find us?" Lini asked.

"I watch. But is something funny."

"What?" enquired Norbert.

"Is five years now no dogs in Poland. Germany army take all best dogs for guard work, all others they shoot. Is against regulation for Polish family have dog. So why is dog in this village?"

"It's not so hard to hide a dog," Otto observed.

"No, but there is penalty, can be arrested."

"Well, look," Lini said eagerly. "Doesn't that show how safe this place is? If Germans came here, those boys never would be allowed outside with their dog."

Otto nodded in vigorous agreement. "That's right, it proves this place is safe."

"Yes, safe, very good," Andrey told them. "But better maybe we watch. One here" – he pointed to the window – "one upstairs for other side. Change every hour."

"No soldiers have come here since the last harvest – isn't that what you said?" Otto asked Jurek.

"No soldiers, no."

"So what are you worrying about?"

Andrey shrugged. "Is safer, is correct."

Otto stretched out at full length on the floor with his hands behind his head. "I've been watching out for the SS for seven years. My eyes, my heart and my guts are all tired of it. You look out for nothing if you want."

"Norbert, Jurek," said Andrey. "You watch with me?"

"Well, we don't want to fall asleep in here," Norbert replied. "But I don't see why we need a steady lookout system. There doesn't seem to be any reason for it."

"Then I watch alone," Andrey told them without resentment. "Is necessary." He moved to one side of the window.

Norbert shrugged and sat down. "So, Lini, tell us more about Joseph. I'll bet you were a wonderful mother."

Lini started to talk about the way her baby loved to play at hiding and how he would cover his eyes when he was found. It was not long before Andrey half-turned from the window, cupped his ear and began to listen. Presently, smiling along with the others, he quite forgot about being a lookout. He, no less than they, was impelled by an elemental hunger stronger than logic: the need to be relieved of tension. Existence in Auschwitz had been a daily agonized struggle to control fear and swallow rage, to master burning nerves, to retain equilibrium in the face of limitless horror. There had been not one morning in which they could know for certain that they would be alive at night. Now, in the isolation of this blessed hideout, it was impossible to maintain defences. The pure, softly falling snow, the rural landscape devoid of threat and terror, helped them to feel the ease they craved. To listen to talk about a child was not only sweet: it was sweetly narcotic. Their imaginations followed Lini avidly to her clean, cosy flat, to a walk along the sunlit waters of a canal, to a park where trees and flowers were blooming. Without being aware of it, all of them were beginning to slip into a world of their own making – a private haven stumbled upon by luck, a miraculous way station to the good life of tomorrow. It lay somewhere between heaven and earth, this precious, private world, and the only creatures inhabiting it were four men and two women.

Chapter 4

Thank You, Andrey

I

"I have only twenty years last July," Jurek said with his quick, engaging smile, "so I have small history. I am from Kraków. My father was doctor, professor in university."

"Kraków?" Claire exclaimed. "My Gestapo boss went there on his days off."

"Is near to camp, yes, forty kilometres. From France you travel far to Auschwitz," he added with a little smile, "but for me was only nice, short trip." He paused, and his face sobered. "One week after German capture Kraków, the SS shoot my father. You know why? Not for resistance. Because he is member intelligentsia! It is Nazi policy – kill Poles with education."

"You know that for a fact?" Norbert asked.

"I know! They shoot all professors from our university they find – same in Warsaw, same everywhere. Oh, some they don't shoot, but send to camps. Is same thing."

"And the rest of the Poles were to work for them, eh?"

"Yes."

"It was plan for all Slavs, for my country, too," Andrey put in.

"My German brothers!" Norbert muttered.

"Go on," said Lini.

"Soon then my mother died. She was sick before with cancer, a young woman, only thirty-four. Ah…" He sighed deeply. "My mother was a beautiful woman, and so kind. I loved her very much, I cannot tell you how much. It was hard task to keep from her about my father."

Lini asked, "Did she die without knowing about him?"

"Yes, she was in hospital already. I tell her father was hiding."

"How old were you?" enquired Norbert.

"I was then fourteen."

"No brothers or sisters?"

"No."

"No relatives?" Claire asked.

"In Kraków no, but outside some cousins, farmers. After I bury mother, I went to them. I worked on farm three years. Then, when I became tall, I went to the woods, to the partisans."

"There are partisans fighting the Nazis?" Norbert asked eagerly.

"Oh, yes! We have People's Army fight in many places."

"I knew that," Claire commented. "I heard the Gestapos talk about it."

"I am fighting with them ten months. But in April last year I have spy mission in Kraków. SS catch me without papers after curfew. So then Auschwitz." He smiled. "Now I know farm work, how to shoot gun, how to live in forest, but I am complete ignorant for my ambition. I have ambition to be doctor, to make special work in cancer so no more like my mother will die. It is my dream. But how will man in twenties go back to school with boys of fourteen?"

"Why not?" asked Claire. "There must be millions of boys and girls who have lost their schooling. When the war is over, there'll be ways for them to make up their education."

"You think so?" Jurek asked eagerly.

"I'm sure of it. It will have to be done."

"That makes me very happy. It is my big dream."

"It's a fine dream," Lini told him with a smile of maternal appreciation. "I'm sure you'll realize it."

In a musing voice Claire said, "I'm just thinking about something. People—"

"Ah," Lini interrupted, "here comes philosophy. I know the signs."

"Shut up," Claire told her affectionately. "I was thinking about how different people are. Lini and I are such good friends, but our dreams of the future are just the opposite. You know what Lini wants to do? She wants to bring up her child so he won't know she was in a camp. The word Auschwitz will never be spoken in her home – she even intends to have the tattoo removed from her arm."

"I will, too!" Lini stated positively.

"Shake," said Otto. "I feel the same way. I want to forget my six years like you do a bad dream."

"And I feel exactly the opposite!" Claire exclaimed with passion. "I won't ever wear long sleeves again. I *want* people to see my number."

"They'll probably think it's your phone number," Lini remarked with a touch of bitterness.

"No, they won't, because I'll tell them what it is! For the rest of my life I'll talk about Auschwitz and Fascism. I'll talk on street corners if I'm able. I'll write articles and send them to newspapers. What did we suffer for to let people forget it?"

"Good for you!" Norbert cried out vehemently. "That's my idea, too! To clean my country! To clean its heart, its mind, of Nazi dirt."

"Some job!" Otto commented with a guffaw. "You can have it!"

"I want it! What else have I lived for?"

There was a moment of silence.

"And you, Andrey?" Claire asked. "What's your dream now?"

He hesitated, groping for words. "My people… know what is Fascism. They know… with their dead. For my people I hope make music. You don't know… how tired is Russian people."

2

"And this," Andrey said to Claire, "I am sure you know: the *Toccata in C* by Bach."*

"I think so. I'll tell you when I hear it."

Andrey began to hum, half sing, in a voice that was untrained, but which could carry the melodic line and was charged with feeling. Sitting cross-legged, he had been giving a concert for the past half hour. With absorption and complete lack of self-consciousness, he was bowing with his right hand, while the fingers of his left moved up and down his chest pressing unseen strings.

He was absorbed, but Claire noted that when he finished each piece his eyes automatically went to her, his smile was for her. Now that Lini had alerted her, she felt a growing electricity in the air. Norbert's glance was steadily on Lini, and she would return his gaze, then look down at Claire's legs, which she was massaging, and then cast a half-glance at Norbert again as though helpless to keep her eyes off him. Jurek, rather strangely she thought, lay on his back with closed eyes. She would have expected him, with his good looks, to be flirting with Lini, but she welcomed the fact that he was not. The one who troubled her was Otto. With a sullen look on his sharp-featured face, his eyes kept darting from Norbert to Lini, to Andrey, to herself. It was obvious that he sensed two couples forming, and felt left out and acutely resentful.

"Otto," she said with deliberation as Andrey finished, "do you think I could have a piece of sugar?"

He smiled immediately and gave her two lumps.

"You know why I asked for it? So I can get strong enough to have you waltz with me the way you did with Lini."

With his nervous laugh he said, "I'll be waiting." The sullen look had left his face.

"Ay!" Andrey exclaimed suddenly. He spoke to Claire in rapid Russian, asking if Jurek could bring him a flat board. He gestured: "About so high and wide. With such a board I can give my fingers real practice."

"I know," Claire told him. "Isn't that what many artists do when they're travelling?"

"How do you know that?" he asked eagerly.

"I had a boyfriend once who was studying violin at the Conservatoire. He used to tell me things about musicians."

"Claire, how much we have in common!" he exclaimed with naive delight. "Music is my life – even in dreams I sometimes play. How wonderful that you like it and understand so much about it!"

"Perhaps less than you think," she answered with restraint.

"Hey, what's all the Russian about?" Otto interrupted.

Wincing inwardly, Claire smiled at him. "Andrey would like Jurek to bring him a board." She explained the reason and told Jurek the dimensions.

"I ask Karol tonight."

Norbert said, rubbing the stubble on his face, "Is there any chance Karol could lend us a razor?"

"I ask."

"I hope Karol won't get sick of us," Claire said, "but I have something on my mind, too. These shoes of mine are starting to go to pieces. Is there any chance—"

Jurek, speaking in Polish, interrupted her. "I'll tell Karol's sister you're French and ask her to lend you her ballet slippers."

Claire burst out laughing. "Thanks. I'm sure every farm woman has dozens of pairs."

"Hey, what's the joke?" Otto asked petulantly. "Let us in on it."

Claire explained. Then, continuing in German, she asked Jurek what size feet Karol's sister had.

He shrugged and grinned. "I look at everything very close, but her feet no."

"How old is this sister, anyway?" Otto asked.

"Is too old for me." There was a mischievous look in his eyes. "Is nice-looking woman, but have thirty years about. Name is Zosia."

"Married?" Otto persisted.

"Her man is war prisoner, work on farm in Germany." He turned to Claire. "Is good maybe I see how big your feet is."

Claire asked Andrey in Russian if she could take off one of the hay boots.

"Let me," he said, "so I can fix it up again."

Jurek laughed heartily when her narrow, rather small foot was exposed. "That is not foot of farm woman. We must look for little girl shoes."

"I don't think the toes are swollen any more," Claire exclaimed with delight. "And the colour is normal. Do you see what your massage is doing, Lini?"

"The colour is better, but still not normal," Andrey said. "Tell Jurek he doesn't need to look for shoes exactly your size. It will be better if he can bring some a little large, but also some cloths that we can wrap around your feet to keep them warm." Claire translated, and Andrey began to fashion the boot again.

Norbert, at the window, suddenly called out. "There seems to be a road about five hundred metres away." Lini, Jurek and Otto joined him. In the distance, clear against the snow, was a wagon drawn by two straining horses, the driver hunched over on the open seat. The sky was a muddy grey now, and the moon had already risen, a whitish globe with a haze over it.

"Wonder where the road goes?" said Otto. "It's strange there's no German transport on it."

"Thank God for big favours," Lini commented. "But the road from here runs straight towards it, so it must go to some town."

"Ask Karol tonight, will you?" Norbert said to Jurek.

"Yes, but is no worry. Not even aeroplanes pass here. You notice?"

"That's right," Lini exclaimed. "By God, we're lucky!"

3

"So!" said Andrey. "Now the other one." Claire was standing, and he was kneeling in front of her, his long-fingered hands moulding the hay deftly around her foot.

"You remind me of a baker with dough."

"I learnt this from a peasant. They know many things about getting along in cold weather. Are you remembering to move your toes?"

"Yes". And then, with a surge of feeling: "You take such good care of me! I appreciate it, Andrey."

He looked up at her suddenly, his liquid, dark-brown eyes conveying so much emotion that she felt disconcerted. "I like taking care of you. In just one day you've become very dear to me, Claire."

"Thank you," she murmured, and covered her unease with a smile. "What part of Russia do you live in?"

"The Ukraine – Krivoy Rog."*

"A small town?"

"Oh, no. Before the war it had two hundred thousand, with much industry. Where did your grandfather come from?"

"Smolensk."

"Why did he leave Russia?"

"He didn't want to do army service."

"You know, even if I had lived under the tsars, I would not have left. I can't imagine being happy anywhere else."

"That's how I feel about France. Are you a communist, Andrey?"

"You mean a party member? No. To try to be a first-rate musician was difficult enough for me. It took all my time."

"But you believe in the system you have?"

"Socialism? Of course. Capitalism is anarchy – it doesn't make sense!"

Claire laughed. "Oh, how my husband would have argued with you!"

Andrey look up in surprise. "You married a capitalist?"

"Not quite. A chemist."

"Do you come from a rich family?"

She looked at him slyly. "Will you stop talking to me if I do?"

Andrey laughed. "It would be educational to talk to a capitalist."

"My grandfather's been a baker all his life, and my father's an optometrist. I'm sorry to disappoint you."

He laughed again and patted her foot. "You can sit." He sprawled down by her side. "Does your family know you were in Auschwitz?"

"I'm sure they don't. They knew I was arrested and then deported, but that's all." She laughed a little, sadly. "In the last year I've played a silly game very often. I write a letter in my mind to my father or my mother or my grandfather, and then I make up their answers. They tell me how their health is, what Paris is like, what they have to eat. And they write me such long letters, too... Isn't it crazy?"

"No," he said gently, smiling. "I think most of us had to use mental tricks to keep going. I've played more imaginary concerts than I could give in a lifetime, every one brilliant. In the worst moments in Auschwitz – like a long count – I've had the world at my feet and the critics in ecstasy."

Claire smiled. "Do you have a family, Andrey?"

"My parents and two younger sisters."

"Are they all right?"

"I don't know. The Germans captured our town early in the war. We took it back only a year ago. I wrote, but there was no answer, and then I was captured. It's three and a half years since I've heard from them. I can only hope they were evacuated."

"Is your father a musician, too?"

"Oh, no. He didn't even learn to read until I started school. We used to study reading together. He's a simple man, a very good man. He works in an iron foundry."

"So how did you happen to turn to music?"

"My parents tell me that before I could walk I used to sway my body when I heard music. At five I was having violin lessons."

Both of them looked up. Otto was standing beside them, frowning with resentment. "I suppose," he said peevishly, "you've been telling him all about yourself while the rest of us you keep in the dark?"

"But I haven't—" Claire began, and was interrupted by Andrey.

"What is matter you?" Andrey asked directly. "What is wrong we talk Russian? I no say you no can talk German."

Otto became a bit flustered. "Well... you understand German, but we don't know a damned word of your language. It isn't fair to the rest of us, that's all."

Claire said soothingly, "Andrey's been telling me about his family and his work. Would you like me to tell you?"

"Well, sure, why not?"

It was a lie, and Claire knew it, and knew that he had no interest whatsoever in Andrey. She said to herself, "This is bad – I ought to stop talking in Russian." Yet, a moment later her spirit rebelled and she thought with resentment, "*Merde*, I've been bullied enough! Who is Otto – an SS man I have to bow down to? I like talking to Andrey... I won't stop. To hell with Otto!"

4

As soon as dark came, Jurek departed for Karol's house. The others amused themselves for a little while by guessing what supper would offer. When this palled, they called upon Andrey. "Intermezzo by Goyescas,"* he told Claire. "Very Spanish, very romantic." The moon, riding a third up the sky, had lost its haze. It was a fingernail smaller than the night before, but very bright, and its rays were beginning to penetrate the room. One by one they wandered over to the window, left it, wandered back again. Presently Andrey stopped playing. Conversation was desultory: their need for food was taking command. When an hour had passed, Otto asked with irritation how long it took to boil potatoes.

"Not this long," Lini told him.

"So where's Jurek? He's supposed to get back here before there's too much moonlight."

Of a sudden, because of this question, their precious, private world began to crumble. Jurek was their lifeline. Without him they would be naked in a world of dogs and SS men. Where was he?

Norbert stood by the window. Otto and Andrey paced. The two women, wrapped in a blanket, lay close together, communicating their anxiety in low tones.

"I know where he is!" Otto blurted out. "He's run! He's found some family that'll take him in, and he's left us hanging."

There were instant protests from the others.

"Then where is he? There are no Germans around – we haven't heard any shots... where is he?"

Norbert said quietly, with irony in his voice, "When Jurek comes back, we'll find out what happened. Meanwhile, friend, think what you like, but keep it to yourself."

"Andrey, please," Claire said, "play something."

"What would you like?"

"The Beethoven Ninth* with full chorus."

He laughed. "Let's have a game. I'll do the cello theme from something by a French composer. You guess which one."

"All right."

"This special, command performance I dedicate to your lovely blue eyes – and to a good supper."

"I accept the dedication only because the eyes came first."

"If I were hungrier, they wouldn't have come first."

Claire laughed and asked, "Aren't you worried about Jurek?"

"Not yet."

He began to "play".

"Oh, I know that!" she exclaimed after a few minutes. "It's a trio by Debussy. Am I right?"

"It's a trio, quite right – by César Franck."*

Claire burst out laughing.

"Ah, Claire, when you laugh like that I get an image of what you'll be when you're in full health again – a very vital girl full of the joy of life. Isn't that how you were?"

"Perhaps so."

"Did you love your husband very much?"

"Yes, very much."

"I'm so sorry he's dead, but you must have given him great joy when you were together."

"Please… it's painful for me."

"Yes, that was stupid. Forgive me."

"Don't worry about it. Start the César Franck over, won't you?" And then, to herself: "Oh, I like this man! I wish I did have normal feelings. That's what *should* happen when you get out of a concentration camp – you should be able to make love right away."

5

A good part of the room had become softly illuminated by the bluish rays of the moon. Andrey suddenly stopped humming. "How long is?" he asked. "Two hours?"

Norbert, peering out the window, answered. "Almost, I think."

Changing to Russian, Andrey asked Claire to translate his thoughts to the others. He felt they shouldn't wait any longer, but go looking for Jurek. He was worried not about Germans, but by the possibility of an accident. Jurek might have fallen into a ditch, or slipped on some ice and broken a leg. One or two of the men ought to go searching for him.

"One man and myself would be better," Claire commented. "I'm the only one who can talk Polish. We may have to go to Karol's house."

"All right. Let it be you and me."

"Norbert is stronger than you are."

"Please – if you go, I want to be the one with you."

"Let's see how the others feel." She began to translate and, almost at once, was interrupted by a cry from Norbert.

"He's coming!"

There was a rush to the window. Talking excitedly, they watched Jurek approach. He had the food basket in one hand and a board in the other. Seeing them in the moonlight, he gestured with the board. They followed Norbert as he went to the door.

"Damn it, he could have been seen every step of the way in this moonlight," Otto said nervously. "From a kilometre off, too."

"Thank God he's safe," said Lini. "That's the most important thing."

Norbert, in the vestibule, had his hand on the knob of the outer door. "No talking until we have both doors shut," he told the others. He admitted a smiling Jurek, who now was wearing a cap at a jaunty angle, and who said gaily, "Razor I have – there is no shoes yet for Claire... here is cello—"

He was interrupted by both Otto and Norbert. "What happened? Where have you been?" Setting down the basket, Jurek pushed the cap back on his head and laughed softly. "You permit me tell lie?"

"What the hell kind of a question is that?" Otto burst out. "We've been goddamned worried about you! Did you see any Germans?"

"No Germans."

"So where have you been all this time?"

Again there came the soft delighted laugh. "Dear friends, please excuse me. Karol was not in house. Zosia, his sister, is very nice woman. She is not too old for me."

There was an instant of silence – and then a wild explosion of laughter from the others. It was an outburst of relief, of amusement at the way Jurek had phrased his revelation, and of excitement. Suddenly now sexuality was vibrant in the room, and they no longer were a family, but three men and two women.

"Oh, that Lini!" Claire thought. "She knew it all right."

6

Handing Claire her supper plate, Lini leant down and whispered in French, "If I were alone with Norbert now, he'd ask me, I know it."

"I'm glad you're not alone."

"That's an unfriendly thing to say."

"No, it isn't, Lini. Look: Jurek's no problem now, because he's found a girl. I don't think Andrey is, either, because he's getting romantic about me for some reason, and I'm sure he'll understand my condition. But Otto will jump out of his skin if you and Norbert get together. He'll make trouble, I'm sure of it."

"We may be dead by tomorrow night. It's ridiculous to talk of trouble."

"I don't think we'll be dead, so it isn't ridiculous. Can't you take it a little slower? Once the Russians get here—"

"It's easy for you to talk, because you have no feelings yet. I need to know I'm a woman again. I've never needed anything so much in my life."

"Lini, dear, the others are waiting."

7

The meal was sumptuous: whole beets, which they ate with the keenest relish, exclaiming over their sweetness; boiled potatoes with the skins left on; a small portion of dark bread; coffee made from acorns – unsweetened, lukewarm, but delicious after the foul brew of the camp.

"St Karol, St Karol!" Otto exclaimed with a belch of pleasure as he swallowed his last mouthful. "Excuse me, Claire, I didn't mean to interrupt. But what a meal, eh? Go on with your story."

"Well," said Claire, "this will show you how carefully the Germans prepared for the war. In order to get his degree, my husband had to do a work of original research and publish a thesis on it. It was something on the chemistry of petrol. After that he went into a different field altogether, soil chemistry." She paused to take a mouthful of food. As usual, she had eaten more slowly than the others, and her plate still was half full. "When the invasion came, we were living in a village outside of Paris where Pierre was working. He hadn't been called up to the army, because he had a mild heart condition. Like everybody else, we ran south. Pierre wanted to get to French Tunisia, but we couldn't arrange a crossing. So, after the Armistice,* we went to Grenoble, where there's a university. He got a teaching job there."

"In what part of France that?" asked Andrey. His hand was cupped behind his right ear, and he was listening with great eagerness.

"Vichy France – the free zone that the Germans didn't occupy until two years later. Now, this is the interesting part: about four weeks after the Armistice, we got a visit from a Vichy official – a collaborator, of course. He told Pierre the Germans had been looking for him from the moment they took Paris. Some research institute in Berlin had studied his thesis on petrol. They were offering a good salary if he'd come there to work. Pierre refused, of course. Then it became really interesting. The salary offer went up. Pierre refused again. The collab tried flattery – he'd be working with important scientists... he'd become well known.

Pierre said no. Then the man shifted to patriotism. France and Germany had become allies now, he said, and it was the duty of all Frenchmen to cooperate with the New Order. Pierre answered that the two countries were allied like a lamb in a wolf's belly." Claire laughed a little. "That made the collab furious, and he called Pierre a communist and a pawn of the English. So Pierre called him a *maquerau* for the Nazis. That's the French word for 'pimp' – a really nasty name. It was a mistake, because the other man was big and strong, and Pierre weighed less than I did. Poor Pierre got a bloody nose out of it."

"Bravo for Pierre," said Jurek, laughing richly. "We Poles got lots *maqueraux* too."

"What happen then?" asked Andrey.

"Nothing. We wondered if there'd be trouble from the Vichy police, but they didn't bother us. However, about every four months someone would come from the government with the same proposition. It was clear they still had Pierre on their minds. Then—" She interrupted her narrative with a little cry: "Jurek, did you get a mirror?"

"Yes, I have it."

"Why didn't I think of it earlier? There isn't enough moonlight now to see by – or is there? Try, won't you?"

"Is not enough," Jurek said, but he got up and crossed to the far side of the window. He took a small mirror from his pocket, moved it from one position to another and returned to the group. With a little laugh: "Tomorrow you be fatter."

"I bet I will be. I'm sure I've gained half a kilo at least since we came out of the hay. I feel so much stronger."

"How about some massage?" Lini asked.

"That would be fine. Please."

"So go on with the story," Norbert said. "You don't know how interesting it is to hear what went on in a country like France. Otto and I don't know a thing."

"Where was I? Yes, we stayed in Grenoble until the end of '42, when the Americans and English invaded North Africa. The

Germans used that as a reason to occupy the free zone. We were eating breakfast when we heard the news over the radio. We didn't say anything – we just looked at each other – and I thought to myself, 'Pierre has to run.' Then I got sick and vomited. That's what I always used to do in a crisis." She added as an afterthought, "Not any more, though: Auschwitz cured me of that." She paused for quite a long moment, but then resumed talking in a calm way, as though the recital no longer had the power to affect her emotions. "Well, we gave ourselves half an hour to decide what to do, but even that turned out to be too long. German army intelligence had already telephoned the Vichy police in Grenoble. They came to the door while Pierre was packing his suitcase. The moment I heard the bell, I was sure it was them. I told Pierre to run out the back. After he did, I let them in. I was telling them some lie about where Pierre was when the back door opened again and there he was handcuffed. They'd surrounded the house."

Norbert asked, "Did your husband know why the research he'd done was so important to them?"

"They never told him. He didn't feel it was anything important – just another thesis by a young chemist. We could only guess that in some way it fitted into work going on in that institute. Pierre used to say the institute must think he knew much more than he did."

"They arrest you too?" asked Andrey.

"Yes." Claire set her plate of food aside. "They wanted me to persuade Pierre. We were taken to prison in Toulouse. You know how? In an army staff car with two very polite, very cultured officers speaking elegant French. And we got lovely treatment at first. My family was notified and told to send us food packages. Once a week there were talks with these two officers – Pierre alone or me alone, sometimes both of us. This went on for six weeks. Then, just after Lini left, the food packages stopped, and both of us were put into solitary on bread and water, not even light in the cells. After a week of that came the final session, in which they just asked, 'Yes or no? If you say no, you go to a concentration camp, and your wife does too. And don't think you'll come back.

You won't!' When Pierre told them no, one of the officers said, 'You answered without asking your wife. Maybe she'd rather be comfortable in Berlin.' Then Pierre said something that made me very happy, even in a moment like that. He looked at me and smiled, and said to the officer, 'If you respect your wife, you don't ask her silly questions.'"

Andrey sighed. Obviously moved, he murmured in Russian, "I have great respect for your Pierre – and for you, my dear Claire."

"So then Auschwitz, eh!" said Otto. "What happened to your husband?"

The reply was quiet and controlled. "He died in Birkenau a year and a half ago."

There was no comment, and no formal expression of sympathy from any of the others. Most who entered Birkenau had died: comment in the face of that reality was, for these survivors, meaningless. After a moment Norbert said, "I've been meaning to ask – you two girls were in the same commando. How is it you're in different shape physically? You both ate the same, didn't you?"

"Claire had two attacks of typhus one right after the other," Lini replied. "First she had intestinal and then, when she was getting better, they put a spotted case in the same bunk with her, so she got that too. She really oughtn't to be here. God likes her."

"And those boils I had last summer," Claire added with a wry laugh. "Almost worse than the typhus. But this one here – I think she's the only one in Auschwitz who never got anything serious. Scabies once, that's all."

"We Dutch are stronger than other people," Lini remarked with a grin.

"She can tell that lie to anyone else," Claire said, "but I handled the records on camp deaths. Tell me, friends, how did any of us live through it physically and mentally? Why is it we didn't all go mad? Norbert, how did you last so long?"

Norbert's answer came out of the gathering darkness. "The only answer I know is that human beings can take much more hardship of every kind than you ever realize. But I personally was always lucky. I never was in the type of commando that killed men off in a month. I'm a carpenter, you see. In all three camps I was in they needed new barracks, houses for the SS, a lot of things. To get work out of us they had to give us enough rations so a man could climb a ladder and hammer nails. So that's how I made it physically – by luck. Mentally, of course, is something else again. No matter what happened, you had to keep your will to stay alive. I'm not the kind of man who has enough words to explain it right. You go through so many different stages... But you girls had two years – you know some of it."

"And you, Otto?" Claire asked.

"Luck, too. In Mauthausen I pulled a soft commando, the hospital. Besides, they let us Austrians get food packages from home. In Auschwitz I was in the kitchen, so I had the chance to organize. But I'll tell you something: the big trick, the hardest thing, was to stay swimming for the first few months. That's when most gave up and died – ain't that right, Norbert? They just couldn't take it."

"Ach, enough of this talk!" Lini exclaimed with sudden vehemence. "Why do we want to go back to the camp? Haven't we had enough of it? Andrey, play us something."

Claire said, "Wait, Lini. I have a question..."

"I smell philosophy again. Postpone it."

"This is serious. I want to ask—"

"All your philosophy is serious. Are all French beauties so serious?"

"Shut up, or I won't let you massage me any more."

"Yah, yah. The big question is what city is more beautiful than Paris? The answer is Amsterdam. Friends, I invite you all to a reunion in Amsterdam after the war."

"My question is," Claire persisted, "would we do it over again? I mean – if we could have known in advance what was ahead of us, would we still have done the thing that got us arrested?"

The room became very still. Then, almost with anger, Lini said, "How can you ask a question like that? We never know the future when we do anything. It's a question that has no meaning."

"No, Lini," Norbert said quietly, "it has meaning. But who can answer it honestly? It's the most terrible question any one of us could be called on to answer."

"Goddamn, I can answer it!" Otto cried violently. He jumped to his feet. "I didn't accomplish one stinking thing for myself or the world by my big socialist speeches." A sobbing note came into his voice. "Give me the chance over again and I'd keep my damn mouth shut." He suddenly began to shout at the top of his voice. "*Nothing was worth my six years. What misery! What hell! What hell!*"

"Quiet! Keep quiet!" Norbert was on his feet, both hands gripping Otto's shoulders. "Get hold of yourself."

Otto said nothing further, but all could hear his stifled, inner sobbing.

"Please, please," Lini said with tears in her voice, "let's make a pact – no more talk of the war, no more talk of the camp. My God, we're free – let's only think of good things now, of life, of home…" Her words turned into sobs. Claire embraced her, whispering, "Hush, Lini, dear. I'll make that pact with you. I'm sorry."

Andrey spoke up suddenly in an ebullient tone: "What is wrong me? Now I have cello, why I don't play? I play you now by Mendelssohn* something. You will see – into here it will bring sun and home and dancing. You listen now."

With the board between his knees he began to play.

8

When they were wrapped in their blanket, close together for warmth, Claire whispered, "I've changed my mind, Lini. Each one of us has the right to do anything we want – anything. Why don't you wait until the men are asleep and wake Norbert up? He's on the far end there."

"Yes," Lini said with a muted laugh, "I know where he is. But I won't do it."

"Are you afraid the others'll know?"

"I don't give a damn about that."

"Then why not?"

"He has to ask me. I can't ask him."

"He must know you like him – why do you suppose…" She didn't finish.

Lini chuckled softly. "I think that after so many years he doesn't quite know how to go about things with a woman."

"Advice from France to Holland: ask him about himself – show him you're interested."

"I'm sure there are some things a wicked Frenchwoman like you could teach me about enticing a man, but not something as simple as that. I began this morning."

"When? I didn't hear you."

"You were asleep."

"So what did you learn about him?"

"He's from Rostock. That's in the north of Germany, a seaport. He did construction work."

"Married?"

"Yes."

"Why was he arrested?"

"We didn't get that far. Goodnight, Claire, I need my beauty sleep."

"Goodnight."

"You know what I'm picturing before my eyes right now?"

"You and Norbert, naturally."

"No. Something pure and spiritual."

"So tell me."

"A beautiful Edam cheese."

9

Suddenly in the night the rolling thunder of an artillery barrage became audible in the room. Claire heard it because she had not been sleeping, and she sat up to listen. After a few moments Andrey was awakened by it – despite his impaired hearing, he was nervously attuned to the sound of cannonading. The others slept on.

Slipping out of the blanket, Claire crossed to the window. Outside all was tranquil – white snow gleaming under moonlight, a placid, starry sky. She turned at the creak of shoe leather. Even in the darkness she knew it was Andrey by the shape of his ill-fitting coat. He joined her at the window with an excited whisper. "You heard it, eh?" He peered out. "The front's moved closer. There's been a breakthrough."

Claire moved to his left side so she could whisper into his good ear. "How far are the guns?"

"Maybe fifteen kilometres, perhaps a little farther." He suddenly caught his breath. "Ah – Katyushas!* The high notes – do you hear them?"

Claire listened, hearing nothing except the distant boom and roar, a kind of pounding in the heavens, she thought.

He held up a finger, waiting. "Now!"

She caught it then above the pounding salvoes – a series of razor-sharp, staccato sounds pitched very high, each following the other with intense rapidity. "Yes! What is it?"

"Katyushas, our rocket guns. We might be able to see them from the other side of the building – they have a fiery tail. You want to come?"

"Yes."

He took her hand, and they moved slowly to the door at the rear. In the main cavern of the building there was more light – the moon's radiance was slanting in through windows in the far wall.

"Why does it make that screaming sound?"

"Rockets travel about eight times as fast as an artillery shell. Katyusha's a terrible weapon. I know from German prisoners how afraid of it the enemy is. Watch for flashes in the sky," he added as they reached the window and he peered out excitedly. "It'll look like a comet."

In front of them was the wood through which they had walked two nights before, the trees tall and black. The bright sky was serene; puffs of white cloud were visible.

After a few moments Claire asked, "See anything? I don't."

"I don't either. Our angle of view is too limited."

"Perhaps they're farther away than you think."

"No!" He was very positive. "Not when we hear Katyusha like this. Ah, what a wonder she is! We even have a song about her."

"Do you want to watch for a little? We may see something."

"You're not too tired?"

"I'm tired, but I haven't been asleep. I've been restless."

He turned from the window and gazed at her closely. "I can guess why – the talk about your past life and your husband."

"Maybe so."

He hesitated, then spoke very earnestly. "Claire, I'd like to ask you something intimate. You don't have to answer. May I?"

"Yes."

"This afternoon, when I mentioned your life with Pierre, you asked me not to, you said it was painful for you. But this evening you spoke about him as calmly as though you didn't feel anything. Forgive me, but it seemed strange."

Claire said nothing.

"I don't want to offend you."

"You don't."

"My mother used to say that those who can't weep can't laugh. Such control as you had this evening violates the heart."

"Yes and no," she told him slowly. "In these two years I've wept a river of tears when I was alone, or with Lini. But in my commando, if I hadn't learnt control, I would have been dead ten times over." She paused for a moment. "Or mad! But I wanted to live – I had a purpose. So it's not hard for me to be controlled as I was tonight. I felt I ought to keep the atmosphere as easy as I could. Look how unpleasant it was when Otto lost hold of himself."

"What commando was it?"

"The Political Department. In Auschwitz."

"As interpreter?"

"Yes. And as a secretary. My boss was second in command of the Gestapo."

"But how could you have been in Auschwitz? Everyone said it was a men's camp only."

"There was one block for women. It was walled off from the rest. The Gestapo needed typists, clerks, secretaries, the way you do in any administrative centre. We never saw the men – they never saw us."

Andrey hesitated, then asked what was on his mind. "Claire, since you were so isolated, how can you be sure Pierre *is* dead?"

She didn't reply for a moment.

"Would you rather not talk about it?"

"No, I'll tell you." Her tone took on a bitter frivolity. "Should I tell you controlled or uncontrolled?"

He said with deep earnestness, "I would like you to feel that you can be any way you want with me."

"I was only joking."

"But I wasn't."

Gently: "I know that, Andrey."

"Tell me."

She turned, and gazed out of the window, and spoke quietly. "The name of my boss was Schultz. He made weekly reports to Berlin on various matters. One of them was the number of prisoners – how many admitted, how many transferred, how many dead."

"And you made out those lists?"

"No, but sometimes I had to refer to them. One day Schultz had an urgent enquiry from Berlin about a prisoner. I looked him up, but he wasn't listed in any of the camps. Yet we did know he had come into Birkenau only three weeks before. So Schultz went to what he called the 'Selection' file. He pulled out a folder and said, 'Probably he didn't last long. See if he's been sent up the chimney.'"

"What?" Andrey exclaimed. "He used the word *chimney* in speaking to you?"

Claire turned to look at him. "Why are you surprised?"

"In Birkenau the one thing a prisoner *never* could do was mention the words 'gas' or 'crematorium' or 'chimney' where a guard could hear you – it was a death sentence if you did."

"Yes, I remember that now. But in our commando everything was in the open. The Gestapo didn't care what we knew, because all of us working there were supposed to leave by the chimney. It's just an accident we weren't liquidated at the end."

"My God," Andrey muttered. "What you've been through!"

"Less than others, much less," she said quietly.

"Tell me the rest."

Claire turned back to the window. "In the folder there were the names of everyone selected for gassing in the two weeks before. Every list had a date. My husband's name was on the second sheet." She paused for a second before going on. "Something happened when I saw it that I'll never understand. I didn't faint, because when I came to myself I was still sitting at my desk. But I went blind. I couldn't see his name any more, or any light in the room. I don't know how long it lasted – five or ten minutes at least. I got back my sight when I heard Schultz calling to me. He said, 'What's the matter with you this morning? Why is it taking you so long to look over a few lists?' So I told him! I said, 'My husband was gassed four days ago.' He looked at me then as though I were an idiot. 'So what about it?' he asked. 'That's how you'll end too – don't you know that yet? Hurry up, now!'"

Neither spoke for a while. Presently Claire turned from the window and said in a low tone, "So, you see, that's how I learnt control."

"Oh, Claire!" Andrey muttered with intense feeling. "My dear Claire." He stared at her, and his lips moved, although no words came, and one hand raised towards her face as though he were about to caress her, but then paused midway. Abruptly he burst into low, urgent, passionate speech. "Why should I hide what I feel? I've never wanted so much to put my arms around a girl as I do now with you. You don't know what tenderness I feel for you, Claire. I want to comfort you – help you forget what happened." He grasped her hands and leant down, trying to see her eyes in the faint moonlight. "But I want to be more than a friend. I haven't been able to think of anything but you since we met. You're like a magnet to me, Claire. No other woman has ever touched me so deeply." He brought her hands to his lips and began to kiss them feverishly. "I want you for my wife, Claire dearest. I promise you all the love that's in me. I know we can have a good life together. And there's nothing like music to heal the heart. Yours needs healing, I..." He didn't finish. Claire was weeping, the tears in her eyes and on her cheeks glistening faintly in the moonlight. He took her face between his hands. "Why have I made you cry? It hurts me terribly to see it. Have I been so wrong? Don't you care for me at all? I felt you did."

"Oh, yes," she told him emotionally, "I like you very much, Andrey. But what you don't know is that inside me I'm dead. I can't begin to think of marriage to you or to anyone."

"Dead? You with your bright eyes, with the way you talk, the way you are? Why do you say that? It's nonsense."

"No, Andrey. I talk and I laugh, but everything's been drained out of me. Not only from my body: from my spirit. I just want to go home, the way I did as a child when I got sick in school, and have my mother put me to bed and take care of me."

Gently Andrey put his arms around her. "Claire, my dear, lean your head against me, please. And listen to me." With a little sigh Claire rested her head against the coarse cloth of his coat. He began to stroke her cheek. "I understand how tired you are. But you're far from your home." He laughed softly. "Mother is far, but Andrey is near, and Andrey wants to take care of you. Soon, I think, my comrades will be here. There'll be doctors to examine you, and good borsch to eat, and vitamin pills, and a bed somewhere to sleep in – and in a week or two you'll feel altogether different."

"And so will you," Claire said bluntly.

"What do you mean?"

"About me."

"No, I won't, Claire. Oh, no!"

She raised her head to look at him. "Andrey, I don't want to hurt you, but to meet a Mussulman like me, and on the second

94

day feel you want to marry her... no, it's not real. It's a fever in you after Auschwitz – your hunger for life. You need the love of a woman – that's so natural – but you're not in love with *me*."

"I am," he said quietly. "And I'll admit it does hurt me to have you say this. But I'm even more glad you're speaking openly."

"Andrey, if I were more attractive and you wanted me physically, that would be normal. I'd want that with you too if I were a little stronger. But love has to grow. It doesn't happen overnight. Not love that means anything."

"Ah, so the French have rules about love, eh?" he said jestingly. "We Russians consult our hearts."

She was silent.

"Claire, tell me only one thing: you do like me?"

"Yes, Andrey, very much."

"Good! Now I'll give you something to think about: you say what I feel is unreal – the fever of a deprived man. But why did I turn to you from the first? Answer that, little Mussulman! Why not Lini? Physically, she's more woman than you are. Yet why do I want to have you in my arms, not her?"

Claire gazed at him with wonder. "The way I am, Andrey... aside from liking me... do you really want me?"

She was startled by his kiss, even though it was gentle. When his lips released hers, she began to weep quietly.

"Now you've learnt, haven't you?" he whispered. "And you'll also learn that what I feel isn't a passing fever. But I see that'll take a little time. I won't mind."

"Oh, Andrey," she said intensely, "I wish we could make love now, right now. But I can't."

"I wish it too," he whispered. "I ache for you."

"I couldn't bring anything to it. Please understand."

"I do, my dear."

"I want so much to feel passion again, but until I do, it would be terrible for me to make love. It would violate me."

"I understand, Claire."

"Oh, I like you, Andrey! I thank Katyusha for waking us up."

"Are you tired now?"

"Yes, very."

"Do you think you can sleep?"

"Yes."

"Come."

At the door she paused, and felt for his face in the darkness, and kissed him quickly. "Thank you, Andrey."

Chapter 5

The Song of Katyusha

I

At first grey light, Otto and Norbert awakened to find that it was snowing heavily. The white curtain outside the window was so dense that they scarcely could see beyond the factory yard. The cannonading had stopped – only a whistling of winds was to be heard. "Hey, you know something?" Otto whispered. "We're free!" Norbert grinned and winked.

One by one, with the exception of Claire, who slept on, the others awakened. They swung their arms to warm up, rubbed chilled hands and exclaimed exultantly over the luck that had brought them to this blessed shelter.

Lini's eyes had gone to Norbert as soon as she sat up – to find his gaze already upon her, his look soft and caressing. It made her heart sing, and she thought to herself, with fond impatience, "You lummox, if you let one more night pass, I'll ask you in spite of myself. But you shouldn't make me do it. It's bad for a woman's pride."

Jurek, fingering his cheeks, said to Otto, "Today we can shave. For me is big necessity." He smiled. "Zosia does not like rough beard."

"You lucky bastard," Otto commented with naked envy. Then, with lowered voice, almost feverishly, "How is she?"

The reply was bland. "Her health is good."

"That isn't what I mean."

Jurek laughed.

"Is she pretty?"

"Not pretty, but nice face."

"Big here?"

"Medium."

"Thin – fat?"

"Medium."

"So how was it? Tell a man something."

"I am gentleman. To talk such things is not, like Andrey say, correct."

"Balls!"

Jurek laughed.

At breakfast, in telling the others about the artillery barrage, Andrey avoided mention of Claire. He knew what was going on with Otto, and he wanted no looks or intruding questions.

"Only fifteen kilometres?" Norbert asked immediately. "That means the German lines are still closer to us, no?"

"Is not for sure," Andrey replied. "Maybe enemy here, our tanks break through there, enemy move this way…" He was gesturing with both hands to indicate the fluidity of the fighting. "Maybe now my comrades is more close to us than Germans, but tomorrow is change."

Jurek crossed himself and said jestingly, "Please, God, no change. Bring Russians here quick, with plenty caviar and vodka."

Casually, smiling, Otto said something that he had been rehearsing since they sat down. "Jurek, you know what I thought when you didn't come back from Karol's? I thought you'd run out on us."

Jurek grinned and extended the palms of both hands. "I am sorry."

"After all, no one could blame you," Otto went on in a light, pleasant way. He kept his eyes averted from Norbert, who had, he knew, begun to stare at him. "You're Polish. All you'd have to do is find a family willing to take you in. You'd be safe then – a lot safer than staying with us." He smiled.

Jurek gazed at him for a moment. "I think you ask me serious question, no?"

Otto shrugged. "Just sort of talking."

"Is more!" Jurek's tone was a mixture of resentment and amused chagrin. "You want find out if will desert you, no?"

"I didn't say that, old man."

"Underneath you say it! So now I tell you!" He pointed to Norbert. "When I have only nine years, he is already in concentration camp. And you" – to Otto – "when I am fourteen. You think I desert two comrades who fight Nazis before I even know what Nazis are? Or desert this two girls and Russian soldier? No! I am Polish patriot – I am not coward, I am not deserter!"

A bit flustered, Otto mumbled, "Excuse me. I didn't mean to hurt your feelings. But it's good to know we can count on you."

There was a moment's pause, and then Jurek burst out laughing. "You was just talking, eh?"

2

The dream was always the same. It did not come each time Claire slept, but when it did, there was no variation in its main images: a small boy rolling a red ball on the ground – rolling it, running after it; a faceless robot in grey-green uniform watching him; and Claire herself, off to one side, gagged and in chains. The dream always ended as the robot, with metallic hands extended, walked towards the boy. Invariably Claire awakened with a tormented cry, as she did now, and lay moaning, heartsick, her body in a sweat.

Andrey reached her before Lini did. "Claire, what's wrong?" he cried. He dropped to his knees by her side. "Are you in pain? What is it?" She didn't reply, but her moaning stopped. Her eyes were shut – she was breathing heavily. "Claire, what can I do for you?" he pleaded, and began to stroke her arm. Lini, reaching them, whispered, "She's not sick: it's a dream she has – it tears her to pieces. Some mornings I could hardly get her up for work."

Claire's eyes did not open, but she muttered, "I'm awake. Please don't talk about it."

"I didn't intend to. You want to rest a little?"

The reply was a heavy sigh.

Lini gestured, and Andrey moved off at her side. "She'll be herself in a little while."

"You know what is dream?"

"It's about something she saw a few months ago."

"What was, please?"

Lini shrugged. "You can imagine."

"Please, is correct you tell me."

She looked at him slyly. "Why?"

He hesitated, and then said with a candid smile, "Claire is now for me very important."

"Then I'll tell you something. I know Claire. When you're very important to her, she'll tell you herself. She wouldn't want me chattering about it." She pointed to Andrey's board. "Why don't you play something for her on that cello of yours?"

"Ah, yes," he responded at once, but he was frowning and obviously dissatisfied.

Laughing at him a little, Lini added: "My general advice is: take it slow."

Otto, entering the room, said, "Hey, Lini, we made a tour of the whole factory. You know what we found? You'll never believe it. It's empty. Ha-ha." He held out his arms. "Let's dance."

"I want to wash the plates now."

"You can do that any time." He took hold of her arm. "Come on, please."

"I really don't feel like it."

Otto's eyes smouldered. "You would if Norbert asked you!"

"Yes, probably so," Lini told him deliberately. "That's how it is, Otto."

He flushed, and a look of such dismay came to his face that Lini felt a pang of remorse. "I'm sorry," she told him quickly. "Of course, let's have a dance."

He turned and walked away.

3

The moment Claire sat up, Otto was at her side, bidding her a lively good morning, asking how she felt, pressing a lump of sugar into her hand. She muttered "Thank you, Otto", and stood up with a slightly bewildered expression.

"Hey, lazy," Lini called, "want your breakfast?"

"Not just yet." She exchanged good mornings with Jurek and Norbert, and then turned to Andrey. Her glance was tender, telling him that their intimacy of the night before was alive in her feelings. "Thank you for the music – it was a help. I'm all right now." He nodded and smiled, but his brows were knitted, and he stopped fingering his board. It was obvious that he was irritated by Otto's behaviour.

"Lini," Claire asked, "which one of the pails is the ladies' bathtub?"

Lini pointed. As Claire went to it and kneeled down, Otto sauntered after her. Mentioning the heavy snowfall, he told her how he had loved snow as a boy, and asked if much snow fell in Paris, if she knew how to ski, if she had ever been in Vienna. Each of her brief answers elicited a new question. Claire's face, as she dried it on her slip, showed increasing bewilderment. Only when she excused herself to go to the lavatory did his staccato talk cease. He remained in the doorway, staring at her retreating figure.

It was a piece of clumsy wooing that made the others exchange glances. Norbert said quietly, "Hey, Otto, close the door, will you? It makes a draught." Otto started, turned quickly with a suspicious look, but relaxed at seeing Norbert's bland expression. He shut the door and joined the others with a very casual air.

"So come back to your child," Norbert said to Lini. "Tell me the rest."

Lini began to laugh. "At that age children don't pay much attention to other kids. But Joey and this boy were fascinated by each other. Only, they behaved like two puppy dogs getting acquainted. They circled around each other on the sand…" She caught her breath and fell silent. The cannonading had begun again – a thunderous rolling in the distant heavens as salvo followed salvo from many heavy guns.

"Ah!" Andrey exclaimed after a bit. "Is closer than last night."

"How close?" Jurek's eyes were gleaming with excitement.

"Maybe twelve kilometres, little bit more."

"German or Russian?" asked Norbert quickly.

"No can tell. Maybe is both."

"How did you know they were Russian last night?"

"Because I hear Katyusha. I no hear now."

"Let's listen."

As Claire came into the room, Lini put a finger to her lips, and then pantomimed eating. Claire nodded.

"Sharp, high sounds, you said?" Norbert asked.

Andrey nodded. "Very quick." He whistled in imitation.

Lini brought Claire her plate, sat down beside her and whispered, "They're listening for Katyusha. That's—"

"I know," Claire whispered. "I heard it with Andrey last night." She smiled broadly at Lini's stare.

"You were up with him?"

Claire nodded.

"Anything happen?"

"Not what you're thinking of."

"Was I right or wrong?"

"About what?"

"Did he want you?"

Claire nodded.

"Ha, I told you. How did he take it when you said no?"

"In a way that made me feel very close to him. But there was more to it than just that."

"What?"

"Tell you later. What am I going to do about Otto? This morning he's like a tom who just ate catnip."

"You're a Frenchwoman of experience, aren't you?"

"No experience with hungry men in brick factories."

Lini grinned. "He's breathing so hard because I told him straight out I liked Norbert better."

"Oh, fine! Thank you. I'll put mice in your bed some time."

"He made me mad, Claire, and it popped out. But he would have learnt it sooner or later."

"Later would be better for me in this situation."

Lini grinned again. "But not for me. You can hold him off. Do you want some massage?"

"Not just yet."

"Anybody hear Katyusha?" Andrey asked.

The others shook their heads.

"What difference does it really make whose guns they are?" Norbert reflected aloud. "We know the Russians have moved closer to us than they were two days ago. Nothing else matters."

"Correct," said Otto. "Do I or don't I smell cabbage borsch?" He sniffed loudly. "I do!"

"Jurek!" Claire cried suddenly. "*The mirror!*"

There was silence and sudden tension in the room. Slowly, almost theatrically, Jurek took the mirror from his pocket. It was small, rectangular in shape. He looked around with a faint grin. "Who first?"

Lini gestured. "Claire was the first to remember."

"Is correct," said Andrey with a smile.

As Jurek came over to her, Claire suddenly began to giggle with nervousness. It was a reaction that surprised her even more than it did the others, because it was quite involuntary. She made no move to take the mirror, merely sat there giggling.

"Hey, what's got into you?" asked Lini, beginning to laugh.

The giggle intensified. "Don't... know." Her whole body had begun to quiver.

It was so bizarre a reaction that the others erupted with laughter. As her giggling continued, their guffaws became louder. The room rang with belly laughs – and then rapidly became quiet. Claire's giggling had ceased as abruptly as it had begun. She was weeping now, sitting very still, making no sound, the tears rolling down her hollow cheeks.

"Oh, what a little fool!" Lini cried. She flung an arm around her. "Why are you afraid of looking at yourself?"

"I'll see a Mussulman," Claire murmured. "I don't want to."

"Such vanity!"

Andrey spoke softly and passionately in Russian. "You'll see a woman who is beautiful to me."

Claire responded with a tiny smile of appreciation, but she shook her head.

"My God, what a romantic!" Lini exclaimed. "Jurek, let me have it." Smiling, she raised the mirror to eye level – and caught her breath. Her brows furrowed. After a bit she muttered, "Ach, I never was a beauty, but…" She returned the mirror and said wistfully, "Maybe Claire's right. Maybe it's better first to gain some weight."

Jurek, who was already gazing at himself, reported more cheerfully, "With me is not so big the change. I was not so long in camp, and I had chance to organize." He tilted the glass so he could scrutinize his stubby hair. "No grey, I can still look like student." He laughed and extended the mirror to Andrey. "You want, or you afraid too?"

"No afraid," Andrey replied. His smile turned into a frown of dismay when he saw himself. He shook his head, muttered something in Russian and held out the mirror with an angry gesture.

Otto said nervously, "Your own mother wouldn't know you, eh? Well, Norbert, you or me?"

"Go ahead," Norbert told him with a tight little grin. "I'm not looking forward to it."

Tensely Otto took hold of the mirror. "You can't imagine – ha-ha – what a pretty baby I was." He laughed along with the others, then added, "I'm glad I had a good breakfast. After seven years this takes backbone." He raised the mirror swiftly. An expression of utter bewilderment came to his face. He stared and stared at his reflection – and for a moment turned to Norbert as though asking him to explain the inexplicable, and then glued his eyes to the mirror again. A thin cry burst from his lips. "But I'm only twenty-four!" He began to wail like a man at a bier. "I can't believe it. I don't recognize myself. The last time I looked in a mirror I was a boy. This is a man of thirty-five. Do I look thirty-five?" He turned to the others with a childish cry. "It's awful! Isn't it awful?"

Beneath his words each of the others heard an echo from his own heart – the sterile wish that time could be reversed, that those who died had not, that the evil they had witnessed and the suffering they had endured had never happened. "Oh, Otto," Claire cried with intense pity, "we all look older now. But when you've rested up and gained weight, and have your hair back, you won't look much older than you are."

"I'll look older and I'll be older," he burst out despairingly. "They've stolen my youth, the best part of life – I'll never have it again... I can never live it!" With sick anguish he thrust the mirror at Norbert. He sat down – a small, crumpled figure – and hid his face in his hands.

Norbert gazed down at him. After a few moments he said to Lini, "Give me a straight answer, eh? How old do I look?"

Her tone was very gentle, almost apologetic. "About forty-five, Norbert."

He nodded. "Doesn't surprise me. It's not so bad."

"How old are you?"

"Thirty-seven." He raised the mirror. A long moment passed. "No, not so bad," he said again. "I'm looking at a man who came through alive where most didn't – better men, too. He might have been ashes, but he isn't. They might have castrated him, or left him a wreck from beatings, but he was lucky: it's hard to believe what marvellous luck he had. He can go home now – he can breathe free, enjoy living, work, have a family..."

Otto looked up. "Thanks for the sermon." His tone was sour and unhappy. "It fixes everything up fine."

"You need talking to, you jackass!" Norbert told him severely. "We've all lost years and a lot else. But to hell with crying over it!" His glance went to Lini, and his voice rang out joyously. "In the dark nights we used to say, 'History will bury the Nazis.' Now it's happening, and we're alive to see it. So what's to cry about? Not a damn thing. In this mirror I see a happy man – and that's all!"

"*Sh!*" said Andrey. "Katyusha!"

All heard it, a staccato screeching in the heavens that pierced through the roar of the heavy guns as rocket followed rocket at high velocity.

"So," Andrey exclaimed happily, "that is how Katyusha sing."

With a slight shudder Claire said, "I have a better name for it: banshee."

"Hah?" asked Lini. "What's that?"

"In Irish folklore it's a female spirit that wails at night to tell people death is coming."

"Honestly," said Lini, "your head is stuffed with more out-of-the-way rubbish! Do you want a massage, Frenchy?"

"Please, but a Swedish massage, not Dutch."

Crossing to the window, Norbert asked Andrey, "Don't the Germans have rocket guns, too?"

"Yes, but fire only one rocket, make different sound. Katyusha go fft-fft-fft… one Katyusha can fire sixteen."

"Snow's stopping," Norbert announced – and then, with an audible gasp, "My God!"

There was a cry of alarm from Lini: "What's wrong?"

Norbert didn't reply. He stood gazing outside like a man in a trance. The others rushed to the window.

The flakes were coming down lightly. Except for a thick layer of fresh snow, the flat, untracked expanse beyond the factory yard looked no different than it had the day before. But the road that bisected the fields, some five hundred yards away from them, was now a flowing river of snow-covered vehicles and marching men. From horizon to horizon in their window view, almost a mile in extent, this white river was in slow movement, machines adjusted to the pace of the men on foot. The latter were in close ranks, their bulky garments encrusted with crystal frost. "German or Russian?" was the question that leapt in the mind of each of the six. Almost at once Andrey shouted "*Nyemtsy!*"

"Germans!" Claire translated.

There was a clamour from the others: "How do you know – are you sure?"

Excitedly Andrey began to point: "Fritz Tiger tank… Fritz howitzer… Fritz anti-air gun."

"I don't see any markings," Otto cried. "Where do you?"

Andrey burst into Russian. "Claire, I know the shape of German vehicles and guns. There's no possibility of my being wrong!"

The moment Claire translated, the others fell silent. With fascination and wonder and hot, churning emotion, they stared at the road. It was, for them, an overwhelming sight. In Auschwitz a Norbert might have comforted himself by saying that history would bury the Nazis, but each morning, when they awakened, they were still in a deranged world where bestiality ruled. None of them really had expected to leave that world alive. Yet now, free and safe, they were watching an army of their captors retreat. Hearts pounded, eyes revelled in the sight! They had the need to look, and look again, in order to be sure that it was not a fantasy. And it was strange, so very strange, to hear no sounds from the road because of the steady roar of the distant artillery. It lent an eeriness to that flowing river of white, as though they were viewing it in a silent film.

It was Claire who finally broke the quiet. "Ah," she murmured in a low, passionate tone, "now, if death comes, I don't care. This makes up for everything. We're seeing justice done!"

A laugh began to sound in Jurek's throat. It bubbled out of his mouth like water from a spring, gaily, sparkling with sunshine. He said nothing, merely laughed and laughed, and slowly became quiet.

Again they were silent. Then, of a sudden, all of them were talking at once, venting their feelings like overexcited children.

Otto: "Those supermen march like they're tired. It breaks—"

Lini: "Tired!"

Otto: "—my heart!"

Lini: "They don't know like we do what it means to be tired, the bastards!"

Andrey (savagely): "Planes! Why our planes don't come now?"

Norbert (sadly, bitterly): "Is this the only way Germans can learn? How many wars do they have to lose before they stop trying to conquer the world?"

Claire (giggling): "Otto, do you have any sugar left? They need it."

A burst of laughter on all sides – harsh, venomous, exulting!

Jurek: "Hooray for Katyusha. I will marry her. She is more to me than Zosia."

Delicious, silly laughter! Satiric cackles! Rapturous flights of fancy – on and on. They began to quiet down as an end came to the flow of men and machines. Suddenly, frowning, Andrey left the window. He began to pace the room in an agitated manner. The others, eyes riveted on the last column, did not even notice his departure.

"Snowing a bit harder again," said Otto.

"Good! They should all freeze to death, the monsters!"

"No, Lini!" Norbert said quickly. "Those soldiers out there aren't SS men. They have to be defeated, yes, but you're wrong to lump them together."

Lini's reply was tart. "The soldiers who guarded us on the march weren't SS either. What pity did they have for a woman who fell in the snow?"

"So what's your conclusion?" Norbert asked intensely. "To decide that a whole people are monsters and leave it at that?"

"You know I don't mean Germans like you."

"So who do you mean, Lini? The boys of twenty who were eight years old when Hitler came to power? Do we hang them or re-educate them? The workers who made those tanks and trucks – what do you do with them?"

"I don't know," Lini muttered. "You've thought this all over – I haven't. But my heart—"

Andrey, returning to the group as abruptly as he had left it, interrupted her. "Comrades," he burst out harshly, "I think we crazy! One hour we stand here look, laugh – but why we no think what happen Fritzes come here?" He gestured excitedly to the road. "Enemy is five hundred metre. He come here, we shot."

"What would they want to come here for?" Otto asked gleefully. "The master race is on the run. What they want is to get away from you Russians."

Andrey, a hand cupped behind his right ear, replied almost violently, "Is many reason come here. Maybe put anti-air gun on roof, maybe use for wounded, how I know?"

"So why haven't they come here already?" Otto retorted. "They must have been passing for hours before we saw them."

"Jurek," Norbert asked quickly, "did you find out where this road goes?"

"Ah, yes – to Bohumín.* Is border town between Poland and Germany. Twenty kilometres."

"There, you see?" Otto proclaimed triumphantly. "That's where they're going – back to the dear old Fatherland."

Andrey responded with an inarticulate cry of disgust. In agitation he turned to Claire. "Translate for me! Claire, we're not behaving rationally. I begin to think we've all come out of Auschwitz in an abnormal mental state. We're so tired, and we want so much to feel safe, that we've made this factory into a dream world. With the enemy right outside, we stand here laughing as though nothing can happen to us. That's madness!"

Claire was silent for a moment. She felt shaken and suddenly fearful. *Were* they in an abnormal state? It was a horrifying suggestion. Yet it was true that she herself had watched the retreating columns without any thought of danger. Slowly, very disturbed, she began to translate. The moment she finished, Andrey pointed his finger at Norbert. "You," he said, his voice snapping, "for twelve year in concentration camp, when you see German with gun, you afraid, no? Why you no afraid of German outside?"

Norbert, frowning, thinking hard, suddenly gestured with both hands. "I don't know," he muttered. He gazed with perplexity at the others. "We've got to keep our wits about us – that's a fact."

"Andrey's right!" Lini burst out. "Of course they can come here! What's the matter with us?"

"Nothing's the matter!" Otto shouted. Pallid with anger, he stepped up to Andrey. "Maybe you're a mental case, you ought to know, but don't include the rest of us. So we got excited at seeing the Wehrmacht run! Isn't that natural? What the hell's abnormal about it? We've been waiting years for this day, haven't we?"

"Then you think we safe here, eh?" Andrey asked sarcastically. "Hitler send you letter, promise?…"

"We're not safe anywhere until the Russians come," Otto interrupted with choler. "But have you got a better place for us? There's been no Germans in this village since last autumn. You just saw whole regiments pass by, didn't you? Christ, you're the one with brain fever, not the rest of us!"

Stepping up to them, Norbert said in a calm, hard way, "We'll sit down now and talk it over quietly, eh?" It was less a suggestion than a command, and it had all of Norbert's twelve years of survival power behind it, and both men responded at once. Casting a glance out of the window at the now barren road, Norbert said, "Jurek, keep watch, eh?" He sat down with his back against a wall, rubbed his chin, and for a moment gazed intently at the two disputants. Lini, recalling the Norbert she had seen upon awakening, found the change in him astonishing. His pale-blue eyes, his strong features, had a cold, taut, iron look that was both reassuring and a little frightening. She could take strength from that iron-hard face, but she never would want to kiss it.

"All for one and one for all, eh?" Norbert said softly. "Let's remember that before we get into any cockfights." Again it was more a command than a suggestion. "Otto, I think everything you said was right as far as it went. But you did miss one thing that's worrying Andrey. If it doesn't apply to you, it does to me. All the time we were watching that road, it never even came into my head that one of those tanks might suddenly head for this factory. But there's no international law says it couldn't have – eh, Otto?"

Otto shrugged in assent.

"Did anybody think of it?" Norbert asked. He waited through a few moments of silence, then went on with his appraisal. "Yet that doesn't mean we're all touched in the head – that's going too far, Andrey. Like Otto said, we were excited, we saw something pretty wonderful, eh? But you're right in one thing: we've become too relaxed. After Auschwitz this is a feather bed. We don't want to lie back and go to sleep. So the real question is this: what should we do if other troops come along?" He glanced around the circle. "Anybody got an idea?"

"*Da, da!*" Andrey said at once. "I got!" He lowered his hand from his ear and turned to Claire. Speaking urgently, he told her in Russian that he had three proposals – all of them based upon his conviction that now they were in extreme danger. The factory was too near the road – it was too conspicuous. It had been a fine shelter so far, but it could turn into a death trap at any moment. Therefore his first proposal was that Karol must try to find families in the village willing to hide them. This had to be done at once – Jurek should not even wait for nightfall to see Karol. The safest solution would be six houses, one for each of them. But if only one house were available – to take Claire and Lini, for instance – that would be better than nothing. If possible, all of them should leave the factory as soon as it was dusk. "So now," he said intensely, "translate this far, yes?"

The proposal that Karol seek homes for them was immediately approved by everyone. There was sharp disagreement, however, over Jurek's leaving the factory in daylight. Lini – and, to everyone's surprise, Otto – supported it. Jurek, in severe opposition, argued that it was not only their own safety they had to think of, but that of a man who had befriended them. A stranger walking a hundred and fifty metres in broad daylight and then entering Karol's house might well be seen by more than one in the village. Who knew what the result would be? Furthermore, once they demonstrated that they couldn't be trusted to hold to an agreement, Karol might become frightened and withdraw all help. Norbert, agreeing strongly with Jurek, also pointed out that since no Germans were on the road at the moment, there was no reason to be panicky. In another five or six hours it would be dark.

When a vote was taken, Lini abstained, Otto changed sides, and only Andrey held out tenaciously for his own position. Claire found herself smiling inwardly at the expression on his face. "A bit on the stubborn side, aren't you?" she thought.

Andrey's additional proposals were harrowing to contemplate. He urged that if they saw Germans on the road again, they jump out of a window at the rear of the factory, run for the woods and remain there until the road was clear. Moreover, until homes were found for them, they ought to stay in the woods every night. Otherwise they might be trapped while they were asleep.

There was a protracted silence when Claire finished translating. Dismay was heavy in the room, because the proposals were not without a measure of iron logic. After a while, Lini laughed a little, rather dismally, and said, "The cure is worse than the disease, Andrey. I'd just as soon be shot warm as freeze to death."

Andrey had an immediate answer. The snow in the woods would be much deeper now than it had been two nights before. He could show them how to burrow into it so they would be protected from the wind. They would be cold, but they wouldn't freeze.

"You guarantee it?" Norbert asked with obvious disbelief. "You've had a lot of practice?"

"Soviet soldier make ambush that way," Andrey replied serenely.

"Dressed like us?"

"Warmer," Andrey admitted. "But is correct we do."

"You do it tonight," Otto told him with a laugh. "I'll wait to see what you look like in the morning – if you come back, that is."

"And Claire's feet?" Lini asked. "What'll *they* be like after a night out?"

Andrey winced and cast a quick, apologetic glance at Claire. "Ah," he said painfully, "the feet I forget." He slipped into Russian. "How are they today?"

"They feel warmer, but there's the same aching."

"That may last for some time." He gazed at her with furrowed brow. "My dear, it's a frightful problem – I don't know what to think. We don't want you to get frostbite again, but…" He gestured agitatedly and didn't go on.

Claire said calmly, "Let's look at it this way: I can stay a few hours in the woods, but I'm sure not all night. So I'll just have to take my chances. Yet that's no reason the rest of you—"

"No," Andrey interrupted. "I'll stay with you."

"That's absurd. Why should—"

"No," he repeated. "I won't leave you, Claire."

Tears came into her eyes, and she turned away from him. "That's not intelligent, Andrey."

"I won't leave you," he told her softly. "I just won't."

"Hey, everybody, listen to me," said Jurek. "Why we no do the Andrey idea of yesterday? We keep twenty-four-hour watch, take turns. From here to road is what – five hundred metre? Suppose German leave road to come here? To woods for us is short, only seventy metre. Even if German come in scout car or tank, by time they come, look around inside here, we are hide safe in woods."

Norbert slapped his knee. "That makes sense. Then we fight the cold only if we have to."

"Very good," Lini agreed happily. "Do *you* see anything wrong with it, Andrey?"

"No," he responded with obvious relief. "Is maybe the best."

"Is that what you really think?" Claire asked him in Russian. "Or are you agreeing because of me?"

Andrey smiled. "Only God could tell me. But it isn't a bad solution."

With a burst of gaiety Otto made a pronouncement: "Friends, I'm taking bets! Luck's been with us from the moment we got into the barn, hasn't it? So I'll bet three to one the Russians get here before we have to run once to the woods. Three to one! Who's taking me up?"

"What money are you betting with?" Claire asked with a smile. "The mark won't be worth much when the war's over."

"Who's betting in marks – think I'm crazy?" Otto responded gleefully. "Wiener schnitzel, that's my bet. We settle at a restaurant I know in Vienna. Three to one – take me up, Claire?"

She shook her head. "I never liked schitzel."

"*What?*" Otto exclaimed with exaggerated surprise. "Now then, Frenchy, suppose right now I took out of my pocket a cold schnitzel three days old – ha-ha – with some cockroaches on it? Would you eat it?"

"I'd eat your hand, too," Claire replied.

A moment later, gazing at the others, she asked herself why their laughter was so uproarious. At best her remark had been only mildly amusing. But all were guffawing like spectators in a music hall, and she along with them. "Just to be alive," she thought, "that's what it is. To be alive and free and on your way home."

Chapter 6

The Naked Heart

There was no cannonading, and no Germans appeared on the road, and even the winds had become still. After the eruptive tension of the morning, it was as though both nature and man had spent themselves and needed a period of tranquillity. In the early afternoon, when they sat down to their cold lunch, the slate-grey clouds at near meridian parted like the curtains of a theatre to reveal a bright sun in a tiny lake of spotless blue. The wide mantle of frosty snow instantly began to glitter as though slivers of glass were strewn all over it. Jurek, whose turn it was to watch the road, called to the others. They stood side by side before the window and gazed at the scene with enchantment. This was not the dirty winter they had suffered in Auschwitz, but winter in its purity and beauty as they remembered it from childhood. With keen nostalgia they began to speak of the joys of sledding, of building snow forts and snowmen, of the gaieties of the Christmas season. In the sentiment of the moment, not one of them remembered the disagreeable days that were a part of any winter, or the confusions, tears and gropings of their early years. A bit of sun on a frozen plain had evoked a magical child-hood for each of them.

After scarcely ten minutes, the grey curtains closed as suddenly as they had parted. With sighs of regret, but still smiling, they sat down. Otto, trying to profit from the occasion, whispered to Claire that her eyes were the colour of the deep blue they had seen in the sky. With reserve she thanked him, and then began to wonder about him. He had been so shy, like a sixteen-year-old stammering over his first compliment to a girl. But perhaps that was the truth about Otto – he was twenty-four, and he was sixteen, and he looked thirty-five – and that was too much of a burden for any man.

Andrey, speaking in Russian, interrupted her thoughts. "You know," he said very tenderly, "your eyes are exactly the colour of that lovely blue we saw in the sky."

It took effort on Claire's part not to laugh. He meant it sincerely, and she had too much feeling for him to wound him, but the identical compliment was like farce dialogue in a play. She was grateful when Lini, speaking of Amsterdam on a winter night, provided an excuse to look away.

"You just can't imagine what it's like," Lini was saying with pride. "With the light of the street lamps on the snow-covered canals, it's breathtaking, like a fairyland. Something I'm especially looking forward to is taking my Joey for his first toboggan at twilight along the Stadhouderskade canal. It's such fun, and it's so beautiful!"

Claire's suppressed laughter found an outlet. "The what canal?"

"Stadhouderskade."

"What a barbaric language! No wonder Holland's always in danger of being engulfed by the sea. Nature can't stand the way you Dutch talk."

"*Oui vraiment!*"* Lini answered pertly. "But when a cultivated Frenchman takes a vacation, where does he go?"

"To the south of France, where else?"

"Where else! How is it that when tulip time comes in Holland, you hear so much French being spoken?"

"Probably by Englishmen."

"That's what you say!" Turning to the others, Lini observed with an air of disdain, "That one thinks the cathedral of Notre-Dame is so absolutely marvellous. Some day I'd like you to see our tulip fields in bloom. Just imagine a whole field with thousands of pure white tulips... and right next to it, a field of purple tulips... and next to that, pink or pure black – I tell you, it's breathtaking, one of the wonders of the world."

"Black tulips – actually black?" asked Norbert. "I never saw one."

"We have them. We even have tulips that look like orchids."

"Any that look like violets?" Claire enquired sweetly.

"Yah, yah, laugh. But wait till you visit me some spring. You'll change your tune."

"Lini, dear," Claire said with smiling eyes, "do you want to hear the real difference between Holland and France? It's not the tulips or Notre-Dame or canals—"

"Oh, I know," Lini interrupted, "it's that wonderful, wonderful light in the sky over Paris. No other city has it. It comes straight from God's eyes to you French."

"It's not that, either. It's this: before the war I was in a crowded bus. It stopped sharply, and I fell quite hard against an elderly man standing behind me. Now, if that had happened to you in Amsterdam, what would have come next?"

"What do you suppose? The man would have helped me to my feet – I would have said 'I'm so sorry', and he would have answered, 'That's quite all right.'"

"Exactly. But my man, being French, tipped his hat to me and said, 'Mademoiselle, this much I didn't hope for.'"

All, including Lini, laughed. "You've got a point," Lini admitted with a grin. "Maybe I'll come and visit you in Paris, after all. Do you think you could find me a handsome man in an opera cape who'll kiss my hand?" She sighed heavily. "All my life I've dreamt of it."

"There are always the pigeons in the Luxembourg gardens."

"Pigeon? Is that the nickname for a gigolo?"

"Oh, no. A pigeon is a bird."

"I know a pigeon's a bird. What's that got to do with a man kissing my hand?"

"If I can't find a man, you can always pet a pigeon in the Luxembourg, and it'll make a little *merde* on your hand."

"You!" Lini exclaimed with a whoop of laughter. "It's time I gave you a bath. You're filthy inside and out."

As the men began to leave the room, Andrey paused at Claire's side. He spoke softly, in Russian. "You know what I wish? That it was my right to stay with you when you bathe. Don't misunderstand. It's only that I want so much to take care of you, to be the one you lean on."

For the second time that day, his intense feeling for her, which she couldn't reciprocate, brought tears to her eyes. Half turning away, she muttered, "Thank you, I don't misunderstand."

"Mother is far, but Andrey is near," he said lightly, repeating his words of the night before.

She turned back to him, speaking with impulsive bluntness. "Only, you're deluding yourself, Andrey. You wouldn't enjoy the sight of my starved body, and I'd hate you to see it. You're not my sister or my mother. You're a man who needs a normal woman, a lover, not me."

"No, Claire, you don't understand," he told her with quiet passion. "It's as though I were playing music and you seemed to be listening, but were only hearing an occasional note. I'm trying to tell you that it would give me great happiness to see day by day how your body was returning to normal. Why? Because whatever comes for us, I think of you as the woman I want for my wife. And what man wouldn't find joy in taking care of his wife?"

"Oh," she cried out, "you're too far ahead of me, Andrey, and you're too serious! It's not good!"

"Why isn't it good?" he asked simply. "I find it very good." He left the room, closing the door behind him.

She stood troubled, confused by her feelings, both annoyed at him and responsive. His solicitude, his caressing eyes, were insidious. She knew that they were beginning to kindle something deep within her – a primitive joy at once again being cherished and wanted by a man... even a febrile man blinded to her by his own needs.

2

Alone, the two women removed their kerchiefs, something they had not done and would not do in the presence of the men. It was not quite two weeks since their heads had been shaven clean; each now had no more than a skullcap of delicately soft hair: Lini's auburn, Claire's wheat-blond. Jesting about it, yet inwardly filled with yearning, each asked how much longer her hair had grown since the day before.

"Yours has shot up quite a bit since yesterday," remarked Claire. "Another week and I'll positively have to go hunting for the lice. How's my peach fuzz doing?"

"Good – like a three-day chick, I'd say. Why is it that a man can be attractive if he's bald, but a woman loses so much of her femininity?"

"Don't worry about it. With your kerchief and your clothes you look very feminine. Anyway, it isn't your hair Norbert wants his hands on."

"How do you know? My husband loved my hair – he used to stroke it often. If I say it myself, it was nice hair, thick and long – I wore it in braids."

"I know. You forget it wasn't cut in Toulouse. But honestly, I think you look better this way. You have a lovely cranium."

Lini guffawed. "My friend! Strip, friend, I want to see your voluptuous figure. Oh, by the way, in cases like yours – I'm quoting a doctor – when you start putting on weight, it frequently happens that one buttock returns to normal, but the other stays shrunken."

"How lucky for me! Sophisticated men like that: it's spicy. I'll wear a tight skirt and become the rage of Paris."

Lini grinned and slapped Claire's rear with the wet slip. "So tell me – what took place between you and Andrey last night? He was looking at you just now with his heart in his eyes."

"I know, that's what's bothering me."

As Lini listened, a tender smile came to her lips. She interrupted only once to say softly, "Yes, he *is* a nice man." They had finished bathing by the time the recital was over. "Tell me," Lini asked at once, "when he kissed you, did you feel anything?"

"Sexually? No."

"Did you dislike it?"

"Oh, no. It made me cry. I felt very tender towards him."

"I don't understand you, then. You're fond of him. You liked his kissing you even though it didn't arouse you. Why didn't you give the poor man what he wanted?"

"Because when I make love again, I want to be full of feeling. My needs are important, too."

Lini paused in her dressing to gaze searchingly at Claire. "Suppose Pierre was here and he wanted you?"

"Lini! What a terrible thing to say to me! How can you be so cruel?"

"Because I don't like to see you lie to yourself. I know what you're willing to do for someone you care about."

"Not in sexual matters you don't. Andrey's not my husband. I've known him less than three days – I'm not in love with him… why do you think I owe him that?"

"I don't think you owe him anything. But we're not normal people living on a normal timetable. If we were, I wouldn't feel the way I do about Norbert. And so I don't think it's a matter of how long you've known Andrey. It's something else."

"What, for instance?"

"Yesterday you asked me if I was afraid of getting pregnant. This morning you had your dream. *That's* the needle in you, *chérie*. You'd be different with Andrey if you weren't afraid of consequences."

Frowning, Claire remained silent for a few moments. Then she laughed a little, very unhappily. "You may be right."

"But it's so unnecessary. Neither of us *can* get pregnant."

"Why not?"

"It's elementary. The sperm and the egg have to get together. We haven't menstruated, so we're not making eggs."

"That's not quite so. If I begin to menstruate next week, it means that right now, without my knowing it, an egg *has* matured. So I would be able to conceive."

Lini laughed. "Do you honestly think you could?"

"There's not much likelihood in my physical state, I suppose, but it's not impossible."

"Well, hold on to your needle if you want it so bad, but I'll give you some free advice – tell Andrey. He's very curious about your dream, anyway."

"I don't want to tell him."

"Why?"

"I'm ashamed of this phobia I have."

"What's a phobia?"

"My fear of having a child."

"My God, what a little idiot you are! In the first place, that fear isn't going to stay with you for ever; in the second place, you can't help what happened. Do you think any of us have come out of that hell without some wounds? But after last night, if you don't tell him, you'll be storing up trouble. He can be as considerate as you want on the surface, but underneath he's hungry for you. It's just too unnatural in our situation to say you like him, but he can't have you."

With sudden weariness Claire muttered, "I'll think about it. Let's go out so the men can bathe."

At the doorway, out of her private thoughts, Lini said wistfully, "You know something? Maybe Holland's free now. It might be only a short time until I see Joey again – perhaps only a few weeks. My God, what a day that'll be! My heart'll pound to pieces." And then, abruptly, "If Norbert doesn't whistle for me tonight, he's going to get raped."

"How does a Dutch girl go about raping a man? I never learnt."

Lini laughed. "I'm thinking it out now."

Outside, in the main cavern of the factory, they found Jurek, Andrey and Otto seated on the staircase. "Hey, girls," Otto called, "save us any soap?"

Claire gestured. "A great big piece. You mind that it's perfumed?"

"Certainly I mind. I'd rather do without."

Jurek laughed. "Anybody give you piece soap, you kiss it all over like it was pretty girl."

"Ha-ha – correct!" Otto pointed to the far wall. "See those first two windows, girls? In case we have to run, we'll use those."

"Why those?" asked Claire.

"All the windows here are double. We discovered that the outer section of every one of 'em was frozen to its frame. We had to sweat with Jurek's chisel and my knife to break a couple of 'em loose. We'll test 'em every hour or so from now on to see they don't freeze again."

"Hooray for you men," Lini exclaimed warmly. "We girls never would have thought of that."

"Hooray for Andrey," said Jurek. "He thought."

Andrey gestured. "In my country we are more used these windows."

"Well," said Otto, "now for that long, hot bath." He cupped his mouth with both hands and called up the stairs. "Hey Norbert, you can come down now."

"Why's he up there?" asked Lini.

"Watching the road while you bathed."

"You want us to watch?"

"You don't have to. We'll take turns from in there."

As the men started for the inner room, Andrey said in Russian, "The bath put some colour in your cheeks. It's nice to see it." And then to Lini, "Massage now is correct, yes?"

"Yes, doctor," Lini responded with amusement. As he left, she remarked to Claire, "He'll make a devoted husband, no doubt about it. I can already see you wearing six flannel petticoats through those long Russian winters."

Claire wrinkled her nose. "Don't ever try to make your living as a fortune-teller."

"Say – we'll both have to start thinking about making a living again, won't we? Well, secretaries and translators..." She broke off as Norbert appeared on the landing above them. "How's the weather up there? I suppose the road's been clear, or you would have yelled."

"Saw some crows, that's all."

"What do crows eat in snowy weather like this?"

"I don't know." Reaching the step above Claire, he added, "And I don't care."

Something in his tone made Lini burst into gay laughter. Smiling, Norbert remained where he was. Then his smile faded, and a look of molten longing came to his face. At once Lini's expression became grave. A moment later Claire would have sworn that neither of them knew she was present. Their eyes had locked and were speaking. Norbert held out his hand then, and Lini stood up. There was a flush on her cheeks; her eyes had become incandescent. Without speaking to Claire, or even glancing at her, she started up the stairs.

Listening to their footsteps, Claire tried to ignore the lump forming in her throat. When she no longer heard them, she began to weep with sentiment and prayed that for Lini it would be sweet and good. And then, from deep within her, there came a crashing wave of memory – of the sun-drenched afternoon when she and Pierre had become lovers. Where were his passion and gentleness now, his kind eyes, his warm lips? Snatched from her for ever, burnt into thin ash for Polish winds to blow! "Oh, my Pierre!"

3

Both trembling, neither speaking, they had ascended the stairs. The first floor, unlike the ground floor, was free of the red brick dust, and part of it was partitioned into separate sections. Norbert opened a door to one of these, disclosing a small room that might have been an office. As the door clicked shut, they turned to each other, still apart, not even hands touching.

They had been too long naked before others and themselves to disavow hungers, fears or what they were. Smiling faintly, but with quivering lips, Lini whispered, "What took you so long? Didn't you know I was waiting for you?"

He took a moment to reply. "I was afraid."

Her eyes searched his face. "Of what?"

Again a moment. "Of my manhood."

"Why?"

"So many years without a woman."

Smiling, her eyes luminous, Lini stepped closer and embraced him. "But no one," she whispered, "could be more man than you are."

His arms clasped her then, and a half-sob of disbelief ripped from his throat as he cried out, "I'm with a woman!"

She was not offended. She knew exactly what he meant. In reply she began to kiss his face with quick, tender kisses. And then, in a gesture of elemental sweetness, telling him that his hunger was her own, she pressed a hand between his thighs and lovingly caressed him. He flamed, and with the shock of his first, hungry kiss, there blossomed within her an exultation of the spirit more poignant, more profound, than she had known on her wedding day, or in the embrace of her husband – or even when the mouth of her child had found her nipple for the first time.

4

Emerging from the inner room, Otto spied Claire on the staircase. His eyes darted from side to side as he quickly came over to her. With a tension that had nothing to do with the remark itself, he said, "I was lucky, got first chance at the razor." He hesitated, then thrust a hand into his pocket for a piece of sugar. "Only three more left – here."

Despite her inner discomfort, Claire accepted it with thanks.

With a slight stammer he asked, "Where's Lini?"

She said nothing.

The words burst out fiercely, "With Norbert, eh?"

She nodded then, feeling acute pity for him. She hoped he wouldn't say anything further, but she was not unprepared for what he did say.

"I was arrested at seventeen, y'know!" It was a low mutter – he had stammered over the word arrested. "I had no experience."

●

He paused, biting his lower lip, and she saw a film of sweat on his forehead. "I mean... Christ!... I mean I've never known what it is to have a woman." He drew an aching breath, and his hot eyes searched her face. "Isn't it awful? Look at the life I've had!" His head jerked as he cast a quick glance back at the closed door of the inner room. "Claire, be nice to me, *please*." He seized her hands, his words tumbling out frenetically. "In the barn, when I gave you the sausage, you cried. You said, 'It's the first time in two years men have been kind to us.' *Please*, be kind to me. I've suffered so much – I was just a kid, seven years..."

"But I *can't*," she told him, feeling deep compassion for him. "Look at me, I'm almost a Mussulman... I'm still dead inside. I'm not ready for any man, Otto."

"Oh, don't say that!" he cried. "It's too unfair." Feverishly he began to kiss her hands – and then, seizing her by the arms, "Just let me kiss you... you'll see, maybe—"

"It's true, I swear," she burst out. She was very distressed now, and she quickly added guile to truth: "Even if my husband were here, I couldn't. It would hurt me, Otto – my body's not ready!"

Slowly he let go of her. He stood up, quivering. She gazed with embarrassment and an aching heart at his forlorn face and thought, "A poor little boy who looks thirty-five."

"But when you feel different?" he asked in abrupt challenge. "What about then? It might not be long."

"Let's see."

His eyes blazed. "It'll be me, not Andrey, you hear?"

"Otto, we don't know what'll happen to us from one moment to the next."

"Now, you listen to me!" he cried fiercely. "First Jurek organized a woman, now Norbert has. You think I could take it if you and Andrey..." His face twitched. "I'll kill him first!"

With a gasp she jumped up from the staircase. "*What?*"

"Don't do it to me, I'm warning you! After the years I've spent—"

"Did they turn you into a Nazi?" she interrupted savagely. "You didn't see enough killing? Or did you get a taste for it?"

125

He gazed at her hotly, flushing. "Just don't do it to me. If it'll be anyone, it'll be me."

She stared at him with revulsion and contempt, until her own thought of a moment before returned to temper her: "A poor little boy who looks thirty-five." She sat down. Slowly, bitterly, she spoke to him with her eyes riveted on his flushed face. "We've been such good comrades together... Each of us from a different country, yet we've been brothers and sisters: no prejudices, no stupidities. Everything the Nazis did, we should hate. But now, like a Nazi, you speak of killing."

The label hurt, and he made a half-gesture of apology. "I didn't really mean it."

"And like a capo you speak of 'organizing' a woman. I'll tell you something! A comb, a spoon, a piece of soap – those are the things we organized in Auschwitz. But Lini and I aren't pieces of soap. We'll give ourselves – if we want – to the man we want. No one can organize us."

"Claire, it was just a way of talking," he pleaded.

"It was much more!"

The door of the inner room opened, and Jurek emerged. Otto, not hearing him, said abjectly, "You hate me now, and I don't want you to. I didn't mean it about killing. But I'm not myself. Being free has done something to me. I feel out of control. All of a sudden I want everything..." He stopped as Jurek reached them.

"Where's Norbert?... He don't want bath today?" A moment later Jurek's eyes showed that he had guessed the answer. His glance went from Claire to Otto. "I think," he said, "I think I go see if windows is freeze up again." He walked off.

"Don't hate me, Claire," Otto whispered. "Please don't."

"Don't make me!"

"Maybe Jurek needs help," he muttered. He turned away, thrust a hand into his pocket and, before she could say anything, dropped two pieces of sugar in her lap. Quickly, he went off.

She wanted to smile at the childishness of his gesture, but she could not. She was trembling with anger and foreboding, her mind's eye seeing again his wild eyes, the twitching of his face. His apologies meant nothing. He had a knife – he had seen murder daily for seven years – and he felt out of control now that he was free. She could understand that. All too well! It was this that was so frightening.

5

"But what's wrong?" Norbert had been asking anxiously for some moments. "Did I hurt you? Why do you keep crying?"

As though hearing him for the first time, Lini shook her head. Her eyelids fluttered open. A smile came to her lips, fled, came back again. Sighing, the tears still flowing, she clasped him fiercely. Her lips were moving with her deep need to speak out something, but no words came. Finally she muttered, "Oh my God!" Then, after a bit, "You didn't hurt me." And then at last, "But it wasn't my body you loved, Norbert, it was my naked heart. When you poured into me, it was life itself kissing me." She began to sob again. "Oh my God, what a man and a woman can be together!"

6

"I wish you could see your face now," Lini whispered. They had clothed themselves against the chill in the room, but they were still lying in tight embrace, eyes and hands caressing in unsated delight as they talked. An occasional rumble of artillery in the far distance went unheard.

"Why?"

"It's so kind. It's how you should always look. I was afraid of your face this morning."

"You're joking?"

"No. When Andrey and Otto were quarrelling, and we had to decide what to do, your face became a piece of iron."

"Did it? You never know a thing like that about yourself."

"I understand now. It wasn't Norbert's face, but the twelve-year face." Sighing, she stroked his cheek. "My God, what you've endured! I know so little about you, but I know you're a wonderful man."

He pressed his face to the warmth of her throat. "No, don't make that mistake about me."

"If I were wrong, you wouldn't be the way you are. You think I don't know how some long-timers degenerated? They started out politicals and ended up brutes."

"OK," he said with a little laugh, "I'm wonderful. Now I want to tell you something. I liked you from the first, Lini darling, and every hour more. But I didn't know how you really felt about me."

"Couldn't you see?"

"I wasn't sure. I thought, 'She seems to like me, but when it comes down to it, maybe her skin'll crawl at the idea of being touched by a German.'"

"Oh!" she exclaimed. "Then it wasn't your virility that worried you?"

"A little of that, too – both things mixed together."

She gazed at him gravely for a moment. "The more I learn about you, the more I like you. But why do you carry the sins of the Nazis on your back?"

"I don't. Yet after what's happened, can any Jew look at a German and not wonder if he's anti-Semitic? Didn't you wonder about me?"

She kissed him swiftly. "No."

"Why not?"

"It was clear from the first. I was wearing my Jewish triangle – I had my eyes open. Not only that, but I'm not ignorant. I know very well the first victims of Fascism were Germans like you. The minute I saw your badge, I was full of admiration for you."

"If only the world will remember..." Norbert muttered with a sigh. "I think of the tens of thousands who died in Dachau and Buchenwald, such wonderful men... But I personally wasn't the sort you think, Lini. The heroes were the ones who took up illegal work. Maybe I'd have come to that, maybe not. I never had to decide."

"Why? Weren't you arrested for political reasons?"

"Yes, but it was an accident."

"Tell me."

"Why should I? Right now you admire me. When you know the truth, you'll leave me for Otto or Andrey."

Gently, Lini slapped his face. "You make bad jokes. So... I'm listening."

"A few days after the Reichstag fire, I saw a workmate in trouble. I didn't know anything about him, but I'd been on a few jobs with him. He was running like mad down the other side of my street, and he was bleeding from a head wound. Naturally, I yelled to him. He ran over to me begging if there was any place to hide – the Brownshirts* were after him. I was in front of my tenement – my women were out. If they hadn't been, I would've hesitated. I grabbed his arm, and we ran up to my flat. Somebody must've seen us and tipped the Brownshirts, or else they were so close behind him they figured he'd slipped into some building. They blocked off a few streets and searched every flat. It turned out Karl was important in the Rostock Communist Party, so they thought me important, too. That's it."

"Only, it was far from an accident, Norbert. You could have turned your back on him. Many another man would've done that."

"I know. But something a man does on the spur of the moment—"

"Counts very much!" Lini interrupted. "It shows what he is."

Norbert pressed his lips to her forehead. "Have it your own way. But I don't want you to get any wrong ideas about me. I was just an apprentice carpenter, uneducated, with my mind on money more than anything else. I hardly ever went to a trade-union meeting. You see, it was such an awful scramble for a working man in those days. I had to support my mother, my sister and my wife, and I'd get maybe one week's work a month. I used to go from door to door with my tool kit looking to mend a chair or a table. So my mind wasn't on politics. I didn't like the smell of the Hitler gang, but I didn't understand much. I only started to get educated in Dachau."

She kissed him hard, pressing against him. For a little while they didn't speak. Then, sighing, she asked. "What happened to your family?"

"My wife divorced me."

"Some wife!"

"I didn't blame her too much. We hadn't been getting along well. Besides, when a man was arrested, the Nazis put heavy pressure on the family."

"Your mother and sister?"

"I haven't heard since early in the war. I know Rostock got bombed heavy."

A moment's silence. "It's getting dark outside."

"Is it? I wish I could stop time. Just lie here with you for a hundred years. What colour is your hair, sweetheart?"

"Reddish brown."

"How much do you have?"

"Not quite as much as you."

"Let's see it."

"Oh, no! Not until it's long enough so that I look like a woman."

"If I close my eyes, will you let me feel it?"

"You promise not to look?"

"Of course."

"Kiss me while I let you, and don't stop. Then I'll know you're not looking."

He laughed. "You don't trust a man very far, do you?"

"It's not that, but—"

His mouth closed on hers. She moved her kerchief back on her head, and his fingers touched the silken cap, moving over it in a caress. After a bit he slipped the kerchief back in place.

"Oh," she exclaimed, "it seems to me that kiss was as hungry as your first one. How could that be?"

"So soft your hair is." He began to unbutton her blouse. "It might have been another woman. I'm so glad it was you. I like you so very much, Lini."

"And I like you tremendously, Norbert. Only I wish I were normal physically! My face never was pretty, but my breasts were lovely. I wish they were like that for you now."

"Forget it," he said gently. "You're a dream to me like you are."

"Ah, what happiness!" she murmured. "Kiss me again like that. No, wait! Let me first... turn this way a little... yes. Ah, now, Norbert, now my man!"

For a little while again, in this bare room, they owned sun and stars, sky and earth, everything except their future. And their future was the one topic neither mentioned.

7

In a quick exchange Claire had said anxiously to Andrey, "Be careful of Otto. Don't talk to me privately. Go on watch tonight, and I'll join you."

Andrey had nodded and taken heed. For the several hours since, he had seemed to be wholly absorbed in playing his "cello", although Claire noted that he never turned his back on Otto. She herself, wrapped in a blanket, had been pretending to sleep.

Otto had not spoken to her since their painful encounter. He was ignoring Andrey, and he scarcely had said a word to Jurek. Absorbed in his thoughts, fearfully tense, he was pacing in front of the window. More than once she had seen his lips move in silent speech; occasionally one of his hands made a small, nervous gesture.

At dusk, when Jurek left for Karol's, her anxiety spurted sharply. Yet, after a bit, she became less apprehensive. Otto continued to pace, and he paid no more attention to Andrey than before. She decided that his thoughts probably were on Lini and Norbert – as, increasingly, were hers.

It was not a pleasant thing, she was finding, to be confronted so bluntly with her own inadequacy. She was happy for Lini, yet at the same time she felt lacerated. She never would have predicted this sudden discontent with her physical state, or the eruption of such longings as now possessed her. Despite Otto's threat, she kept fantasying* herself alone with Andrey – she, fearful of nothing, both of them knowing again, after such long deprivation, the high rapture of an impassioned union. She felt angry with her body, furious that no effort of will could command her flesh to come alive.

Jurek, to her surprise, returned in less than an hour. She sat up, yawning for Otto's benefit, and asked what news he had.

"Got you young girl rubber boots. I think they fit. Got tonight no bread, but onion and potato soup, turnips and – what you think? – little piece soap from Zosia."

Otto's nervous laugh rang out. "She's certainly mad about you. How come you're back so quick?"

Jurek grimaced ruefully. "I have devil's luck. Zosia is sick. Got fever, cough."

"Poor you," murmured Claire.

Otto guffawed. "Just once with you, and a girl gets sick, eh?"

Andrey, who had put aside his board, said impatiently, "So tell us… the houses… what Karol say?"

Jurek gestured helplessly. "He will ask tonight. But he think answer is no."

Andrey muttered an oath in Russian. "Why?"

"We have no papers. If Germans come, they ask everybody for passport. They shoot family that hide us."

Again Andrey swore. "Is bad!"

"Well," said Jurek, "now we eat, eh?" Matter-of-factly he enquired of Claire, "We call Lini and Norbert, or no?"

Claire thought about it for a moment. "No. They'll come down when they're ready."

Spooning out the soup, Jurek asked, "Why is so bad, Andrey? We have way to run to woods…"

"You translate, yes?" Andrey asked Claire rather formally. He explained that he had been hoping for a final breakthrough by the Soviet forces close to them. Ever since mid-afternoon, however, their sector had been quiet, and the only guns they had heard were far off, perhaps twenty-five kilometres. If this meant a temporary stalemate in their area, the chances of their being captured were much greater.

When Claire had translated, Otto remarked sourly, "There's nothing we can do about it, is there?"

"I am thinking," Andrey replied.

"Great. If your brilliant mind thinks of anything, let us know. Until then, why don't you stop moaning and groaning about what might happen? All it does is turn this good soup sour in my belly."

"You do not speak to me like comrade," Andrey said slowly. "Why?"

Otto didn't answer.

It became the first meal they had eaten in silence.

Chapter 7

"Three Capuchins"

I

A little while after they finished eating, Lini and Norbert appeared. Lini's first words expressed so much pagan gaiety that even Otto smiled, and the tense mood in the room began to lighten.

"If I look like I'm walking," she announced with a bubbling laugh, "go and see an eye doctor. I'm floating on air, and I hereby testify that Adam and Eve knew what they were doing when they ate the apple."

Welcoming her mood, Claire said jovially, "I always wondered if there was something to it. Is it my turn to spoon-feed you now?"

"Not at all. But I'm starving. What's to eat?"

"Cooked Norbert," said Otto.

The remark produced a howl of laughter, and was followed by a good deal of equally clumsy banter. By the time they settled down to sleep, the harmony of the group had been superficially restored.

Not Claire's inner harmony, however. The events of the day had set up a clamour within her. She was aching to be alone with Andrey now, ready to respond to her feelings, whatever they might be. She was well aware that with most other men, however attractive, it wouldn't have been so. But Andrey had made clear that he wouldn't demand anything of her. She wondered if he knew how wise he'd been – a musician's sensitivity, perhaps.

Almost an hour had passed since the group had settled down. For some time Otto had turned restlessly from one position to another, but now, lying on his front, head pillowed on both hands, he was quiet. She had whispered to Andrey earlier that she would leave the room as though going to the lavatory. He was to follow if Otto didn't awaken.

She slipped out of the blanket and sat up. She waited until she had counted to thirty. Getting to her feet, she waited again. Otto remained still. He was lying between Norbert and Jurek, and she thought she heard him snore, but she could not be positive it was he. She moved, stepping carefully, keeping her legs well apart so that the knee-high boots wouldn't scrape each other. They were well worn, and they made her passage so silent that Andrey didn't become aware of her approach until she was quite close. When he turned, profile to the window, she saw half a face, half a smile. He nodded, and she continued on. Her pulse was racing, and she was very excited, but she took a long time with the door. The hinges were dry, and she paused between each creak to watch Otto's figure. After some minutes, the door was sufficiently ajar for her to slip out. A few moments later, Andrey joined her. He felt for her hand and kissed it. In silence they crossed the dark cavern to the staircase. At the halfway landing he whispered, "We need to be close to the stairs in case we see any Fritzes." He opened a door to the first partitioned section they reached. "There's a window here." She went in, and he shut the door behind them. The room was dark, but there was a shimmer of moonlight at the window. Together they peered out. The bright three-quarter moon was almost at zenith in a sky studded with dark, racing clouds. The road was clearly visible, a thin line between the white fields.

"What's up?" Andrey asked her quietly.

Claire told him, adding, "You saw how he was this afternoon – so tense, talking to himself. I take his threat seriously. I hope you will."

Andrey nodded. "Will you stand here, Claire? I'll be able to see you and check the road over your shoulder."

She stepped in front of the window. "With an unstable man like that, there's no knowing what can make him explode. Even before

Lini and Norbert got together it made him jealous when we talked in Russian. It'll be worse from now on. I think we have to stop it."

There was sufficient light for her to see the grimace of discontent that came to Andrey's face. She felt for his hand. "I won't like it either, Andrey, but I think it's necessary."

"Necessary for your peace of mind, if nothing else, I suppose." He raised her hand to his lips, then pressed it to his cheek. "I agree, no more private talk. But there's something else: his knife. It has to be taken away from him."

"How can you do that?"

"One way or another it'll have to be done. I'll talk to Norbert – he knows him best... So, have we settled this nasty matter?"

"I suppose so. You'll watch out for him, won't you?"

"Of course."

"Damn Otto! Everything's been so fine until now."

"It won't seem important a year from now, or even a week." His free hand reached out, and his fingers caressed her cheek. "I haven't liked today very much. We've had so little time together. Tomorrow will be worse."

"You can play music and I'll listen. That'll bring us together."

He asked softly, "Do you want to feel like that with me – together?"

For a moment she didn't reply. Then she leant forward and rested her head on his chest. He put his arm around her, and she felt him breathe deeply.

"Andrey, I have something to ask you."

"Yes?"

"Let's say Otto weren't here to interfere with us. After a bit wouldn't you resent it if I wouldn't be lovers with you?"

"You told me you aren't capable of feeling yet. How can I resent you for that?"

"You could."

"It would be very stupid of me."

"Except for one thing we haven't mentioned: that a man needs to be passionate to make love, but a woman doesn't."

"Has that thought been bothering you?"

"Yes."

He kissed her forehead. "As I told you today, you don't really understand me. If you ask me whether I want sexual love with you – yes, of course, with all my heart I want it. But that involves your feelings as well as mine. If you were to feel nothing, then our contact wouldn't be love, but a kind of mechanics. So then you'd end up resenting me. Would that be good for either of us?"

"You have your needs. Sometimes satisfying them is more important than anything else."

"That's right, and I'll tell you frankly that I might act differently with another woman. But the biggest need I have now is for you to love me. I don't want *anything* to spoil the possibility of that happening. There are enough obstacles between us as it is."

"Yes," she thought, "obstacles we'll never climb over either – and that's why this is so unfair to you." A wave of feeling swept through her, of affection and compassion for him, of longing on her own part to come alive. She raised her face. "You haven't kissed me."

As on the night before, his kiss was gentle. It was she who tried to turn it into something else, pressing her lips to his, seeking in long contact the elusive spark. It ended in a sob. "I hate myself!" she cried bitterly. "Maybe I'll never feel anything again. Damn Auschwitz, damn the war!"

"Now hush," he told her, stroking her face, "you're being ridiculous. What do you expect of your poor body? Give it a little time."

"I was hoping…" she murmured, but didn't finish. She leant against him. "Are you watching the road? We mustn't—"

"I've been watching. Right now the moon's behind a cloud. Claire, I want to ask something that may be painful for you. It's none of my business, yet I do want to ask it."

"What?"

"Were you raped in the camp?"

She raised her head. "Is that what you think happened to the women?"

"To some of you, surely."

"That was about the only misery we didn't have to worry about. What gave you such an idea?"

"I wasn't the only man it occurred to. You were helpless, why wouldn't the SS use you?"

Claire laughed. "I suppose everybody at home will have the same idea. It's so far from the reality. The SS had all the girls they wanted – the women guards, Polish women who were willing or they bought. But us? The minute we got to Birkenau our heads were shaved… after one night in quarantine we had lice on our bodies – in a week we stank, and half of us were sick. What was attractive about us?"

"Then what's your dream about?"

"Oh! So that's what's on your mind?"

"Claire, dear, that dream is terrible. Why do you have it? What happened to you?"

In the instant following, as she recoiled from his question, she began to fantasy something strange and painful: she was back in Paris, somehow in the room she had occupied as a student. It was a sun-drenched afternoon, and she was lying naked, weeping with frustration, in the embrace of a man whose face was obscured, so that she didn't know whether it was Pierre or Andrey or someone else. And a piercing thought came to her: "The wounded heart can't love." The words sent a shudder through her. She became aware of Andrey again, of his question, and with anguish she asked herself whether she would walk wounded through the balance of her life. Bursting into tears, she pressed her body to his, clutching him as a child in turmoil clings to a brother or a father. Inside her a child's voice was wailing: "Listen to me, comfort me, listen to the awful thing that happened to me!" And then, without willing it, she began to speak in the staccato, compulsive manner of someone in high fever, her voice now rasping, now weakly tremulous, the phrases punctuated by sobs: "In September a transport came to our section. No transports ever came before. Why did this one? I don't know. Seventy-two Jewish children from five to twelve. I saw the document – they'd been hidden by Polish families. Now the Gestapo had them down for the ovens in Birkenau. I watched them from the window. My heart was like a crazy hammer. So innocent and beautiful. There was a conference in my office, and I was sent outside. I couldn't speak to them: there were SS and dogs. One boy had a big red apple. About six years old, nicely dressed, brown hair, brown eyes, so pretty and sweet. He was playing with the apple, rolling it, running after it. The Gestapos came out. They shook hands. All of them went away, except one from my office, Kress. He stood looking at the boy. He walked towards him. He called out in Polish. The little lad turned around. Kress bent over... he took hold of his ankles and swung him... and smashed his brains out against a wall." Claire choked and flung her head back. "But don't think that was all! He put the apple in his pocket. And that afternoon his wife and child came to visit him. He took the boy on his lap... kissed him... and then he said, 'I have something for you' – and he reached into the desk drawer and gave him the apple."

With an inchoate cry she went limp.

2

He had lowered her to the floor and lain down beside her, murmuring passionate words of comfort, stroking her, kissing her wet face. It was some time before her shuddering body became still, before she could stop weeping. Finally, in an aching voice she whispered, "It ruptured something inside me. I'll see that child's face in every child I ever see. I don't think I can have children now. He murdered all children for me."

Andrey said nothing. He stroked her, kissed her forehead.

"You can see that, can't you?" she muttered brokenly.

"Claire, dearest," Andrey said very gently, "I've passed through towns where there were no buildings, no parks, no trees, only rubble and shell holes and stumps, and everywhere dead men. Yet even there I've seen new blades of grass coming up between cracked stones. You need time, Claire. Time for your body to heal – your heart, your mind. You've lived two years in a hell that Dante couldn't have imagined. Give yourself time, darling: nothing is final."

She was silent, huddling against him.

"Dear, sweet Claire," he went on softly, "if I had a magic carpet now, I know where I'd take you. There's a little place on a river bank that's very dear to me. There are birch trees to sit under, and many little patches of wild flowers. The water of the river is so clear that you can see the fish swimming in it, and it sparkles all day when the sun is on it, and it flows on and on like life itself, nothing ever stopping it. And there, if I could play music for you, the deepest music in my soul…"

Andrey stopped, and Claire felt his sudden, physical tension. "What is it?"

"*I hear tanks!*" He leapt to his feet, and was at the window before she could sit up. "*I can't see them, but I hear them!*"

"*Can you see the road?*"

"*Only part of it. Run! Get them to the escape windows. I'll stay here.*"

Andrey's command, and the surge of fear within her, propelled her headlong out of the room. She was at the staircase before she reacted to the darkness and the danger of a fall. She pulled back sharply, grasped the railing and began to descend in the only way possible – each foot feeling its way down to the step below. Her movements were not as slow as her fears made her believe, but in an agony of worry she began to shout before she had reached the first landing: "*Wake up! Lini, Norbert… tanks… wake up… go to the windows… do you hear me? Wake up, wake up!*" She was still shouting as she reached the ground floor and saw the figures of the others bolting from the inner room.

For a moment there was bedlam. None of the four had caught more than the words "wake up", and they were yelling questions as they ran towards her – the men not even knowing in the darkness and their haste whether it was Lini or Claire they had heard shouting.

"Tanks!" she screamed. "Tanks! Tanks!"

The word got through. She heard Norbert's voice: "On the road or coming here?"

"I don't know. Andrey heard them. Run to the windows."

Automatically they obeyed, with Norbert crying out, "But didn't he *see* them?... Where is he?"

"*I hear them!*" Otto yelled.

"They're coming here," Lini burst out in panic.

"Shut up!" Norbert commanded violently. In the few seconds before they reached the windows, all heard the grinding roar of many heavy motors approaching rapidly. Norbert's voice snapped: "Jurek... Otto... open the windows. Claire, where's Andrey?"

"Upstairs! He couldn't see..."

Norbert shouted out in a bull roar: "Andrey – are they coming here?"

Andrey's reply was somewhat muffled, but distinct: "No, they stay on road. Fritz Tigers."

"Can you see clear in all directions?"

"Only half of road. Rest is dark."

"Should we run?"

"Nothing come yet."

"Stay here!" Norbert ordered the others. "I'll look, too." He was off at a run towards the inner room.

Freezing air burst in upon them as Jurek forced open one of the double windows. Out of the darkness came a heavy thump, followed by a gasp from Norbert, who had fallen. He was up, swearing, running again. Jurek and Otto were both pounding the second window now, Otto cursing. It swung open.

"Tanks not coming here!" Andrey shouted. "They pass our road already."

They listened to the terrifying roar, and could detect the sound of passage. "Sound like many," Jurek said. And then, with jubilation: "It means for sure Germans are running from here."

"God in Heaven!" Lini cried. "Maybe the Russians will be here tomorrow! Just think if they come tomorrow!"

They heard a happy yell from Norbert. "They're almost out of sight. There must've been twenty of 'em – monsters, going like hell."

"Can we shut the windows?" Claire asked. "I'm freezing." Weakly she leant against Lini. Her thighs were trembling.

"Why not?" Otto said happily. "All we have to worry about here are false alarms. We're snug as bugs in a rug. Did you feel that cold? Can you imagine if we'd followed Andrey's idea?…" With a hoarse grunt he swung around. He was staring at Claire with his mouth agape. They were about a yard apart, and in the darkness she couldn't see the expression on his face, but she sensed something amiss. A moment later, hearing Andrey's footsteps on the way down, she knew what it was. Her throat tighted,* but she stepped towards him. "Otto—"

"You were upstairs with him!"

"We were talking."

"You liar! You don't have to sneak upstairs to talk."

"I couldn't sleep. We didn't want—"

"Liar, liar!" he cried with rage and hurt. He bent over, hugging his belly with both arms. "Get away from me, you liar!"

"Otto, *please* believe me. I swear it's the truth!"

"Liar! Go away."

Lini seized her arm. "Come on." Weeping silently, Claire followed her.

3

They stood in a group. Claire, speaking in a whisper, was explaining about Otto. Norbert raised his hand and cut her short. "All right, we have to get the knife, no more talk is needed. When he comes in, I'll stand here and ask him for it. Jurek, get over by the door. If he doesn't give it to me, I'll grab him and you jump him from the back. Then you fish it out, Andrey. Agreed?"

"Yes," said Jurek. "But if he come in here wild with knife in hand—"

"Keep a hold on your chisel. Crack his wrist or his arm – don't hit him on the head. Girls, get over to the end of the room. Andrey, what are you doing?"

Andrey had taken off his heavy coat and was wrapping it around his left arm. He said quickly, "Maybe knife stick coat, but not me. I not soldier for nothing."

"Good. Let's get this over with. I'll call him."

"Oh God!" Lini exclaimed in a muffled voice.

Opening the door, Norbert peered out. He called jovially, "Hey, Otto, you still hiding from the tanks? They weren't looking for you, boy."

Otto's voice came back from the cavern in a dry, controlled tone: "Come over here, Norbert, will you?"

There was a moment's hesitation on Norbert's part. "Coming." He walked out.

Lini gasped. "Jurek, go with him."

"Why? Otto is old comrade to Norbert."

"Maybe not now because of me. *Go, please.*"

Jurek slipped out. Andrey went to the door. The two women were holding each other, their anxious breathing audible.

"Andrey, can you see anything?"

"No."

They waited. Lini began to whimper. Then Jurek came in, followed at once by Norbert, who closed the door. "Otto's a bit of a shaky character," Norbert told them quietly, "but he's got some glue in him that holds him together. I've got the knife. I didn't ask him for it. He called me out to give it to me."

"Did he say why?" Claire asked in astonishment.

"He said he was feeling nervous – he wanted me to hold it for him."

"Well! My respect for Otto goes up. But what now? Is he going to stay out there by himself? It'll get very embarrassing."

"If I know Otto, he'll be back after a while with a joke to smooth things over."

Andrey, putting on his coat, asked, "Is everybody ready sleep? Or like little music first?"

"Yes, for God's sake let's have some music," Lini told him. "My nerves are raw. First the tanks, then Otto – this hotel isn't as quiet as it used to be."

"It certainly isn't," said Claire somewhat shrilly. "Let's complain to the manager tomorrow. The service is getting bad, too. The maid forgot to bring clean towels this morning."

"Is it too late to see him tonight?"

"See whom?"

"The manager."

"The manager of what?"

"Claire, what are we talking about? The manager of this hotel."

"Why, you silly, this isn't a hotel – it's a brick factory."

Lini laughed heartily. "I feel better already."

Andrey, board in hand, sat down facing them. "While I make music, who watch road?"

"Whose turn is it after Andrey?" Norbert asked Jurek. "Yours or Otto?"

"Mine." He went over to the window. "*Hey!* I see Zosia."

Norbert bolted after him. "*Where?*"

"In my mind I see her."

Norbert chuckled and cracked Jurek on the back.

"What is the use to watch?" Jurek asked. "It is so dark I could not see Zosia if I was kissing her."

"The moon's been going in and out of the clouds. If someone's by the window, he'll be able to check the road once in a while." Norbert sauntered over to the two women who were side by side with a blanket over their shoulders. Sitting down by Lini, he took her hand in his. She turned to him, smiling, and leant against him. "Concert, concert," he called with a light-hearted zest he had not shown before.

"Ladies and gentlemen," said Andrey, "for number first, I play you old song of Armenian people. Has name 'The Dream'.* Is mother sing her baby to sleep."

"Good," Lini told him. "This baby would love to have you sing her to sleep."

Andrey placed his fingers in position high up on the board. In Russian he said, "This performance, dear Claire, is dedicated to the day when you and I will sit under my birch trees by the river. Do you accept it?"

"With pleasure." A strong impulse made her add, "Sit with you, and put my arms around you, and be your lover."

"Oh!" he murmured with a catch in his breathing. "Ah, Claire, if it'll only come to be!"

"Concert, concert," said Norbert, clapping his hands.

Within a few moments after Andrey had begun to hum the theme, Claire felt she knew why this particular song had come to his mind. The melody was lovely, and its first bars evoked a strong, nostalgic mood, yet there also was an element of brooding sadness in it that was appropriate to their situation. She closed her eyes. Her mind drifted to what she had just said to him. In truth she had no belief in a future that would see her on a river bank with Andrey. Nevertheless, she had wanted to reach out to him, to tell him that her feeling for him was becoming strong.

She began to hum the melody. It was simple, and, in the way of folk songs, already had been repeated twice. She heard the creak of a door and thought, "Otto coming." There was a strange, electric gasp from Lini then, and Claire's eyelids snapped open. Lini's hand gripped her thigh convulsively – Lini's eyes were riveted on something across the room. An inner core of fear conveyed what it was before Claire saw it. Someone was cautiously opening the front door.

For the second time in her life Claire went blind. When her vision returned, a soldier dressed like a Capuchin monk was standing in the open doorway. His uniform was hidden by a white cape that fell almost to his ankles; a pointed cowl covered his helmet; in his white-gloved hands there was a sub-machine gun. Needles of fire stabbed Claire in bowel and heart and brain. She began to scream silently over and over again: "German or Russian?" The soldier took a few steps into the room. He was some fifteen feet from them and had not yet seen them in the darkness. Two others tiptoed in. A hot electric eye flashed and was swung like a whip from one side of the room to the other. There was a surprised grunt from one of the white figures as it caught the group on the floor. A voice shouted harshly, "Hands up!"

They obeyed, each one knowing in that moment the full meaning of the words anguish and despair. The soldier had spoken in German.

"Who are you? What are you doing here?"

Jurek, at the window, still unseen, answered at once in a tone of humility, "We live around here, sir. Just having fun with couple girls."

The flashlight struck and found Jurek smiling obsequiously, hands above his head.

"Get over with them."

"Yes, sir."

"Anybody else in this building?"

"Not that I am knowing, sir."

"Any Russian patrols been around this village?"

"No, sir."

There was a moment of silence. "Walter, report to Dietrich."

"Yes, sir." One of the soldiers left.

"You girls – get out of here, go home!"

Lini jumped up. Claire, body and soul inert, was unable to move even when Lini grabbed her arm. Her eyes were on Andrey's pallid face as his eyes, sad and hopeless, were on hers.

"Well?" the voice barked. "Get out."

"Claire, go!" Andrey said in German.

She was on her feet then, with Lini's hand pulling her rapidly towards the door. In the vestibule a whimper burst from her lips and she tried to turn around. Lini pulled her outside.

4

The shock of the icy air, the sheer fact of being outside, ended Claire's torpor. When Lini said "This way" and began to run to the left, Claire followed at her side, crying, "Where?"

"Karol's!"

It was quite dark. The fresh snow was soft and deep, almost to their knees. Within ten yards both were panting, but neither could stop talking. They were running side by side, yet they were not talking to each other: it was a babbling, a spewing out of terror and anguish they could not contain. "Don't let..." Lini kept repeating. "God, don't let... don't let, God... please, please, God..." And Claire, like a drunkard, "No, no, no, no... too cruel... no, no..."

Sixty yards from the factory, Claire stopped, chest heaving. Lini swung around. "Come on! If they find out, they'll be after us. I'll run in front. You follow me." She started off, and a moment later Claire followed at a forced little dog trot. Neither was babbling any more – two years of Auschwitz had conditioned them. When death came to loved ones, you went blind, or you screamed without control, or you babbled incoherently and wanted to die. And then something happened in the chemistry of your soul and you stopped babbling, and got back your control, and struggled again to survive. Claire's whole being became concentrated on the effort of running. It was easier going now that Lini was breaking a path ahead of her, but her body was pleading its weakness.

A thin beam of moonlight appeared ahead of them, and they saw the roof of a house about fifty yards off, somewhat to their right. "There!" Lini called, and headed for it. A bit farther on, as the cloud cover dispersed a little more, they saw a house on their left that was closer. Lini changed direction again. By the time they reached it, the moon had darkened. Lini, ten yards in advance, began at once to knock on the door. In the still night her rapping sounded frightfully loud to Claire. Yet, when she was standing beside Lini, with the door still obdurately shut, she too began to beat at it with both fists and call in a gasping voice, "*Pani'e* Karol, *Pani'e* Karol!"*

148

To one side of the door, although they were not aware of it, a black curtain behind a window pane was drawn slightly aside. Eyes peered at them. A moment later the door opened a few inches, and a man's voice said roughly in Polish, "What do you want?" They could see only part of a face.

"Are you *Pan* Karol?"

"Who are you?"

With desperation Claire blurted the truth: "From the factory. Didn't Jurek say there were two girls?"

"What country you from?"

"France."

"And you?"

"She doesn't talk Polish – from Holland."

The door swung open, and they saw a thin, middle-aged man.

"I'm Karol. Why did you come here?"

"German soldiers – they told us to get out…"

Karol looked with quick fright towards the factory. "Do they have the men?"

"Yes. Where can we hide?"

"Not here!" He looked again towards the factory and spoke very rapidly. "A tool shed." He pointed. "Straight through those trees. House is locked. I was there tonight, family in Katowice. Bring you food tomorrow night."

Claire turned swiftly. The moon had again partly emerged from the clouds, and she could see a thick stand of trees a hundred yards off. "Thank you… bless you," she said fervently.

The door had already shut.

"There's a place – through those trees."

Without a word Lini began to run. The moon was unveiling, and the area between them and the trees was quite visible now. The struggle began again for Claire: weak limbs against the snow, aching lungs, neck muscles beginning to quiver spasmodically. Her face and body were streaming with sweat; her scalp was icy under the thin kerchief; snow was melting in her boots. Her mind began to repeat an agonized refrain: "Keep going… keep going!"

The stand of trees loomed up about thirty yards ahead – tall, thick-trunked firs, boughs drooping under their burden of snow. The tops of the trees were shimmering in the moonlight, but at ground level there were only a few streaks of light. In that darkness lay security, and both women were spurred on by its nearness. Lini's broad figure trotted forward unceasingly, her bare legs swinging high with each stride. Every ten yards she glanced back quickly to make sure Claire was following. She knew how tired she herself was.

A sound of motors reached them from the area of the factory, but neither woman looked back. Lini came to the trees, and at once was swallowed up by the darkness. Claire, staggering forward now rather than running, made the last few yards to the shadows and toppled over sideways. Lini reached her in the next moment. Dropping down beside her, she lifted her and cradled her head. Neither could talk. The sweat was still pouring out on their foreheads as their hearts hammered and their heaving chests gulped icy air.

The sound of motors was growing louder. It was not like the grinding roar of the tanks they had heard earlier, but it was much closer. Fearfully Claire sat up and pointed towards the factory. Lini stepped to the edge of the treeline, and Claire, still panting, was at her side a moment later. In the moonlight they could see the factory clearly. The road leading to it was alive with long-barrelled guns, with trucks and other vehicles.

"The men!" Lini burst out in a wild, cracked voice. "What's happened to them? How long has it been? Maybe they let them go. Maybe they're only prisoners again. We'll find them after the war. Norbert—"

As though whips of wire had lashed their naked flesh without warning, both women screamed. From the factory, cutting through the motor sounds, had come the crack of several rifles.

5

They stumbled through the woods, weeping, holding each other, inarticulate with agony and desolation. Before Claire's eyes was a tormenting image of Andrey as she had seen him at the last – hands above his head, face hopeless, saying, "Claire, go…" – and between his knees a pine board that had been his dream of the future. "Too much!" her heart cried. "Oh, too much." And Lini, who had known Norbert in love so few hours ago, was stumbling through a delirium in which endlessly she saw him shot and falling, shot and falling.

They saw nothing, knew nothing, except the ache in their hearts. Nor were they aware that the distant drumming in the heavens had begun to move closer as new batteries opened fire. Like a great iron scythe cleaving the sky, the scream of hot metal was advancing towards them. They came back to reality with cries of fear when a dozen white-caped figures stepped out from behind trees. A voice snapped in Russian, "Who are you?"

"Escaped prisoners," Claire gasped. "From Auschwitz."

"What are you doing in these woods?"

"Running from the Germans."

"Where are they?"

"That way, in a factory building. They have cannon, we saw them."

"So did we. Get over by that tree. There are some Katyushas behind us that are going to sing right away."

Claire, body turned rigid, pulled Lini behind the tree. "*The factory. It's their target. They have Katyushas.*"

"They're going to hit the factory?"

"The factory, yes, the factory."

Lini's voice rose in a shout that went unheard as rocket after rocket was launched from somewhere behind them. The tremendous hiss of their rising became a sharp, wild scream as they turned into fiery meteors. "Yes, hit it, hit it!" Lini shouted savagely. But then, all too soon, the rockets were gone, and the Katyushas were silent, and Lini's cry became a whimper: "Dead! The men are dead."

They stood, wordless now, each knowing that without the men they would have been lost, that the men had given them their lives, had made them women again. "Claire, go!" Andrey had said, and the words had meant much more: "Go and be safe if you can in this unsafe world, go with my heart's blessing to find the love and music I wanted to give you. Go, my dear."

"Come along now, girls," a soldier told them. "I'll get you where you're safe."

Clinging to each other, they followed him.

Notes

p. 6, *Bois*: Literally, "Wood" (French). Since the word is capitalized, the reference is probably to the Bois de Boulogne, a large public park in west Paris and a popular picnic destination.

p. 7, *Wehrmacht*: The army of Nazi Germany.

p. 8, *"Los aufgehen!"*: "Get up!" (German).

p. 10, *twilight*: Lighted as by twilight; dim, obscure, shadowy (*OED*).

p. 10, *"Merde!"*: "Shit" (French).

p. 20, *spasibo*: "Thank you" (Russian).

p. 20, *"Da, da!"*: "Yes, yes!" (Russian).

p. 21, *"Nyet!"*: "No!" (Russian).

p. 25, *borsch*: Borscht, a Russian soup.

p. 25, *Debussy*: The French composer Claude Debussy (1862–1918).

p. 25, *Stara Wieś*: A Polish village 143 km north of Auschwitz.

p. 33, *Like a Bruegel painting*: The Dutch painters Pieter Bruegel the Elder (*c.*1525–69) and his son Pieter Bruegel the Younger (1564–1638) were both authors of winter landscapes with people skating on ice.

p. 39, *the socialist revolt we had in '34*: The so-called "Austrian Civil War", also known as the "February Uprising", a series of clashes between the right-wing government and socialist forces in Austria which took place between 12th and 16th February 1934.

p. 46, *'The Blue Danube'*: A famous waltz by Johann Strauss II (1825–99), also existing in a choral version.

p. 46, *Beethoven or Tchaikovsky*: The German composer Ludwig van Beethoven (1770–1827) and the Russian composer Pyotr Ilyich Tchaikovsky (1840–93).

p. 46, *Dvořák... 'Songs My Mother Taught Me'*: The Czech composer Antonín Dvořák (1841–1904) composed this song for voice and piano in 1880.

p. 59, The concentration camp of Auschwitz was not one camp, but a constellation of many camps divided into three sections.

Section I, called Auschwitz, contained the command headquarters and a camp for men – with a few details of women who did special office work and were walled off from the rest of the camp.

Section II, not quite two miles away, was called Birkenau. Here there were both a men's and a women's camp. This was where the gas chambers and crematoria were located.

Section III consisted of different labour camps and factories extending over hundreds of square miles [AUTHOR'S NOTE].

p. 62, *Salope!*: "Bitch!" (French).

p. 62, *Chérie*: "My dear" (French).

p. 73, *Toccata in C by Bach*: Either the *Toccata in C minor* (BWV 911) or the *Toccata in C major (Toccata, Adagio and Fugue in C major*, BWV 564) by Johann Sebastian Bach (1685–1750).

p. 77, *Krivoy Rog*: Kryvyi Rih, a city in central Ukraine.

p. 79, *Intermezzo by Goyescas*: That is, 'Intermezzo' from *Goyescas: Los majos enamorados* ("The Gallants in Love"), a 1911 piano suite by the Catalan composer Enrique Granados (1867–1916), inspired by the work of the Spanish painter Francisco Goya (1746–1828).

p. 80, The Beethoven Ninth: *Beethoven's Symphony No. 9 in D minor*, Op. 125.

p. 80, *César Franck*: The French Romantic composer César Franck (1822–90), author of a famous set of piano trios.

p. 83, *the Armistice*: The Armistice of 22nd June 1940, signed near Compiègne (about 80 km north-east of Paris) by officials of Nazi Germany and the Third French Republic.

p. 88, *Mendelssohn*: The German composer Felix Mendelssohn Bartholdy (1809–47).

p. 90, *Katyushas*: Soviet rocket launchers. Their name literally means, in Russian, "little Katyas".

p. 109, *Bohumín*: A town in the Moravian-Silesian region of the Czech Republic, which had been annexed by Nazi Germany at the beginning of the Second World War.

p. 116, *"Oui vraiment!"*: "Oh really!" (French).

p. 129, *the Brownshirts*: The colloquial name for the *Sturmabteilung*, the paramilitary wing of the Nazi party before Hitler's ascent to power.

p. 132, *fantasying*: Fancying; imagining.

p. 143, *tighted*: Tightened.

p. 145, *'The Dream'*: An Armenian folk song.

p. 148, *Pani'e Karol!*: "Mr Karol!" (Polish).

CALDER PUBLICATIONS
EDGY TITLES FROM A LEGENDARY LIST

Changing Track
Michel Butor

Moderato Cantabile
Marguerite Duras

Jealousy
Alain Robbe-Grillet

The Blind Owl and Other Stories
Sadeq Hedayat

Locus Solus
Raymond Roussel

Cain's Book
Alexander Trocchi

Young Adam
Alexander Trocchi

CALDER

www.calderpublications.com

EVERGREENS SERIES

Beautifully produced classics, affordably priced

Alma Classics is committed to making available a wide range of literature from around the globe. Most of the titles are enriched by an extensive critical apparatus, notes and extra reading material, as well as a selection of photographs. The texts are based on the most authoritative editions and edited using a fresh, accessible editorial approach. With an emphasis on production, editorial and typographical values, Alma Classics aspires to revitalize the whole experience of reading classics.

For our complete list and latest offers

visit

almabooks.com/evergreens

ALMA CLASSICS

ALMA CLASSICS aims to publish mainstream and lesser-known European classics in an innovative and striking way, while employing the highest editorial and production standards. By way of a unique approach the range offers much more, both visually and textually, than readers have come to expect from contemporary classics publishing.

LATEST TITLES PUBLISHED BY ALMA CLASSICS

www.almaclassics.com